Passion's Fury

VIKING'S FURY BOOK 3

VIOLETTA RAND

Print Edition

Published by Dragonblade Publishing, an imprint of Kathryn Le Veque Novels, Inc

For Mom, Jill M., Milisa Z., Phyllys C., Pat B., Meredith M.,
Kathryn L.V., Victoria V., and Jessica F.
all women who have helped shape my future.
Thank you.

TABLE OF CONTENTS

Chapter One

November 867 AD
Trondelag, Norway

HOW MANY PEOPLE could Runa's eldest brother, Jarl Roald, squeeze into the great hall at one time? She eyed the double doors in the back of the room, thrown open in the dead of winter to accommodate the guests that had traveled many miles to celebrate the birth of her nephew, Kollvein. Two lines of well-wishers spilled outside. Additional braziers had been set up in the courtyard, providing much needed warmth for their visitors.

"There are an infinite number of joys to experience in this world," Roald started, his toothy grin, permanent. "But this..." He lowered the fur-swathed bundle in his arms, revealing his newborn son. "Is the greatest of them all."

Silvia, Runa's sister-in-law, appeared then. She, too, carried a similar bundle. "Unless you are blessed with two babes," she added, standing next to Roald. "Eva insisted on introducing your daughter at the same time."

It made Runa smile, for Roald's wife had given birth to twins only yesterday—a boy and girl. Her brother wished to keep it a secret, for some would misinterpret twins as a bad omen.

"Meet Katla," Silvia said, showing off the infant's perfectly shaped head.

Everyone cheered.

"And who will wear the crown?" someone called from the throng.

"Though my beloved wife is capable of many wonders, she didn't deliver my son and daughter at the same time," Roald assured them. "Kollvein kicked his way into the world first, then my sweet daughter arrived." The jarl gazed at his second child with genuine affection. "When the time comes, rest assured, another generation of Jarl Brandr's bloodline will sit on the throne."

"And will you offer these blessed children up for baptism?"

The room fell deathly silent.

Runa pushed her way through the crowd, recognizing the man who spoke. Recently returned from Northumbria, Olvir Olavson had converted to Christianity. All of the Trondelag was abuzz with the news. Anyone who betrayed the gods shouldn't be here. Kollvein and Katla belonged to Odin.

"Get out," Runa hissed as she seized Olvir's arm.

The Norseman gazed at her. "Be quiet, woman. What right do you have to order me about?" He jerked free of her grasp. "This world must change. Otherwise, we will all burn for our sins." He looked her over, disgust on his face. "Especially a wanton girl like you."

Refusing to be insulted, Runa unsheathed the knife she kept at her hip. She held it close to his face, unafraid. "Care to curse me again?"

He chuckled, but didn't make a move to strip the weapon from her hand. The people standing nearby were watching and listening closely.

"I speak only truth."

"Do you?" Runa challenged. "Falsehoods you picked up in a foreign land. Belief in a weak God. Take your stories and go tell them to the wild pigs." Runa shoved him in the direction of the doors. "Do not come back here, Olvir." Her hand started shaking. It surprised her how desperately she wanted to use the knife, to stab him in the throat and silence him forever.

Before she could do anything, someone quickly disarmed her from behind.

She spun around, finding Thorolf, Roald's newest captain. "Be still, Runa. Let me take care of this fool."

Unable to resist staring at the handsome warrior, she often wondered why he didn't have a wife and a dozen children. Thorolf resembled the men from ancient times, his wolf fur cloak worn as a symbol of his accomplishments as a Berserker, his chiseled features and golden hair a complete distraction.

"Aye," she said obediently, lowering her offending hand. "Do with him as you please."

She watched with fascination as he grabbed a fistful of Olvir's collar and forcibly ushered him outside. There was no doubt in her mind why Roald had promoted Thorolf to such a coveted position in his personal guard. He had proven himself invaluable to her family. And now that she thought about it more, he always seemed to appear at the right time.

Good instincts? Or did Odin work through him?

"Now that the troublemaker has been extricated from the celebration, may I suggest we drink and eat, honoring the arrival of my children?" Roald raised his cup. "*Skål*," he offered a traditional toast.

A woman shoved a cup of mead into Runa's hands. "To your family's health and success."

Runa emptied the vessel in one swallow, irritated with herself. The best way for a girl who wanted to serve as a temple maiden to forget a man she was hopelessly attracted to was to indulge in as much mead as she could drink, then lock herself in her chamber where she could sleep.

Chapter Two

THOROLF RELEASED OLVIR once they walked beyond the courtyard where no one could overhear them. "Consider yourself fortunate." He eyed the dissenter, knowing trouble would follow him wherever he went. "Unlike Runa, I will not hesitate to punish you if I see you here again."

Olvir straightened his cloak. "I am helpless against the mandates of my new faith. I must share the message of my new God with everyone I meet. What harm is there in giving free men a chance to choose between Odin and the Christ?"

Roald didn't seem to be the kind of man who'd forgive a captain for mishandling a situation. Especially with a Norseman who had abandoned Allfather. "What you do in your own time is not my concern. But when you are standing on Jarl Roald's lands, you will observe the same rules I do. Keep your radical ideas to yourself. Now, go." Thorolf waved him off.

"You would send me away in the middle of the night without my horse?"

Thorolf sighed. "Payment for your disrespect."

"I am not a man without resources..."

"What are you saying?"

"A small measure of kindness now would be repaid threefold someday."

Thorolf did not like what Olvir was implying. "Are you

attempting to bribe me? To win my favor?"

He shrugged. "I am requesting mercy. Tis a bitter night and I have a long walk home."

"Something you should have remembered before you opened your bloody mouth inside the great hall or insulted Lady Runa."

The man clicked his tongue. "If she passes for a lady anymore."

Thorolf didn't think, he simply acted—pinching Olvir's throat between his thumb and fingers. "What quarrel do you have with the lady?"

"It's a private matter."

"Nay." Thorolf squeezed his neck tighter, knowing it would snap easily if he applied just the right amount of pressure. "Tell me or I'll deprive you of air altogether."

Olvir struggled to swallow. "I've known her since our childhood."

"And this is why you treat her with such disdain?"

"No. Before my sire sent me to Northumbria to train as a soldier, she promised to wait for me."

Thorolf didn't understand. "Wait for you? Instead of your mount, perhaps I should claim your tongue." He released Olvir and reached for Runa's knife tucked in his weapon belt. "Then no one would suffer from your incessant babble again."

"I wished to marry her," the smaller man clarified. "Though she never gave her outright consent, she agreed to consider our union."

"As you've already said. There is no ring upon her finger. And to my knowledge, Jarl Roald is the one you must gain permission from. He is her guardian now. When did you return from Northumbria?"

"Eight days ago."

Thorolf assessed the man more closely, noting his expensive clothes. Not the garments of a hardened warrior. "Did you succeed in becoming a soldier? How many battles did you fight in? How many men have you killed?"

"None."

Thorolf grinned. He knew the answer before Olvir spoke. But he credited the man for being honest. "So you failed as a footman? What good were you to Danes if you cannot wield a sword?" He also guessed the man couldn't wield his pikk, for what woman would fuck a half-man with soft hands?

Olvir leered at him and tapped his temple with his fingertip. "I adjusted to my surroundings. When Prince Ivarr learned of my quick wit and ability with numbers, he hired me as a scribe."

"A lap dog," Thorolf muttered, loud enough for Olvir to hear him.

"On the contrary," Olvir said with confidence. "Physical strength might win the fight, Thorolf, but a keen mind keeps the war financed."

"I care little about what's behind the battlefield." Thorolf stepped closer. "But I know Jarl Roald would never accept you as a husband for his only sister. And I never gave you permission to use my name."

"I didn't realize I needed it." Olvir stood his ground.

"Go, before I change my mind about what to do with you."

"I want my horse."

Thorolf sighed in frustration. The man was as persistent as a fly. "Leave. Now." He poked Olvir in the chest for emphasis.

"I will be back. My claim on Runa holds merit."

Anger swirled just below the surface then, for Thorolf deeply admired Lady Runa. More than that, the idea of this inferior creature touching her, even dreaming about her, made his stomach turn. "There will be no further contact between the two of you."

Olvir chuckled. "You are a soldier, not a member of the family. When it comes to deciding..."

Thorolf didn't need the finer things in life ... didn't care a fig for speaking as eloquently as a skald or priming his mind to be a scholar. He knew one thing and head-butted the nag, knocking him on his arse. "*Argr.*" He waited for Olvir to stop writhing in pain before finishing his thought. "Stand up like a man." He'd not give him another chance to leave on his own accord.

Olvir staggered to his feet, his forehead wet with blood. "What did you call me?" He sucked in his cheeks.

"Did I stutter? *Argr.* You are every bit unmanned—womanish."

No insult cut deeper.

"I challenge you," Olvir said, his scowl as humorous as his fighting stance.

"And what will you defend yourself with?" No weapon hung at his hip. "A bone used to carve your words?" He laughed violently. "I am tasked with protecting the jarl's family. And as long as I draw air, you won't set foot on these lands again."

Thorolf shoved him down the footpath. Olvir nearly lost his balance, but Thorolf didn't care. He did it again and again until they'd gone some distance from the longhouse. The full winter moon shined overhead, casting the world in silver light. He stopped abruptly then, memorizing Olvir's features.

"The next time you expect a girl of fifteen seasons to keep her word about *waiting for you*, perhaps you should consider speaking with her father or guardian first. A man wouldn't hold a child to such a severe promise."

Olvir spat on the ground. "She's no longer a child."

"Aye," Thorolf agreed. It pained him to envision her—so beautiful and strong willed—perfect in every way. "And after her reaction tonight, I think you have your answer."

Done wasting his time, Thorolf turned his back on Olvir, ready to return to the celebration and get drunk.

Chapter Three

THE MEAD RUNA consumed took the edge off her self-doubt and loathing. Instead of retiring to her chamber, though, she followed Thorolf outside. At a good distance, of course, for the last thing she needed was for anyone to know how she felt about the captain, especially him. She'd witnessed the confrontation between Thorolf and Olvir, privy to every bitter word exchanged. She had to cover her mouth to keep from gasping aloud when Thorolf head-butted her childhood friend for questioning his authority.

The captain's fierce loyalty and fearlessness not only impressed her, it set her restless heart on fire.

Olvir was the only son of Jarl Otkel, a minor chieftain from an ancient family. She didn't know what consequences would follow for Thorolf striking a future lord. Though a freeman, he did not possess noble blood. But in Thorolf's defense, he'd done what any warrior should, sent the arrogant weakling home with his tail tucked between his legs.

Marry him?

The idea made her want to laugh and scream at the same time. Yes, she'd been infatuated with Olvir as a young girl. Odin forgive her. He seemed so clever back then, gifted with a deep singing voice and the ability to weave words together like a skald.

The time apart had been hard at first. She dreamed of him often. But after a year had passed, her feelings cooled and she opened her heart to the gods, knowing where she belonged. North. Beyond the borders of the jarls. She sighed, thinking of the great temple tucked in the forest where only suppliants of Odin were welcomed until the Thing was called to order.

There, the chieftains and freemen of the north settled important regional affairs, feasted, and offered blood sacrifices to the gods. Every five years, the grand council assembled at the temple, and it was there Runa hoped to declare her intention to become a maiden. She had five months to anticipate that day.

Until then...

She stopped walking. Surely, Thorolf had been too involved in his own thoughts to notice her following him back to the longhouse.

"Step out of the shadows, Runa." He didn't bother turning around.

She did as he asked, leaving the cover of the tree she'd hidden behind. "How did you know?"

"I know the sound of your footsteps."

"Even in the snow?" She didn't believe him.

"Weight and size make a difference." He pivoted, meeting her gaze. "And those boots..." He looked at her feet. "Bells couldn't give your location away more."

She frowned, then stared at the precious gift her Sami sister-in-law, Eva, had given her a month ago. A pair of reindeer skin boots, embellished with fur and gold stitching. "These are fine boots. Warmer than any pair I've ever owned."

"And dangerous," he said. "For no one in the lowlands wears a similar pair. I could track you like a fox would a rabbit."

"I'm curious why you know so much about me, Captain Thorolf." She waited for an explanation but got none. "Let me guess—tis your duty."

The annoyed look on his face pleased her immensely.

"Eavesdropping is not an admirable habit for a lady to have."

"Do tell, Captain Thorolf, what is then?"

He folded his arms across his broad chest. "Weaving. Stitching. Singing."

She giggled. "Not habits," she corrected. "Those are treasured skills."

"I'd rather see you bite your fingernails than go unescorted late at night."

His genuine concern touched her in a place she carefully guarded. Her heart belonged to Odin—to the idea of becoming a temple maiden. Not to Thorolf or any other man. "That will be enough from you, Captain." She started to walk by him, but he caught her arm and pulled her back. "What are you doing?"

"What I should have done earlier." He let go of her arm, but blocked her path to the house. "Why did you threaten Olvir? Do you think you're strong enough to kill a man of his size? Any man?" He pulled her blade from his belt. "This is a paring knife, meant for fruits and vegetables, not to maim someone."

She reached for the weapon, but he refused to give it to her. "I am sure if Jarl Roald wished you to own a weapon, he would have provided you with one."

She arched a brow. "My brother would do no such thing. He likely fears I'd stab him in the middle of the night."

His throaty laughter wrapped around her like a warm blanket, heating her insides. "So you're a dangerous one?" He eyed the blade, then her. "Perhaps I should return this to the kitchens."

She shrugged. "Do as you must, Captain. I'll only fetch another in the morn. I prefer being armed. This is a dangerous place."

"Aye." He offered her the blade. "If you'd allow me the privilege of getting you a real one."

She smiled. "You'd do that for me?"

"Tis my duty to keep you safe."

That was the last thing she wanted to hear from the ridiculously handsome warrior. She'd rather he kissed her and held her close. "Thank you."

He rubbed his chin. "For what?"

"For getting rid of Olvir."

He nodded. "The past has a way of catching up, doesn't it?"

"A very much unwanted past," she admitted.

"I cannot account for your taste in men, Lady Runa. But as long as I am within earshot, no one will insult you without answering to me."

There he was again, the honor-bound Thorolf. Though she truly appreciated it, she wanted to see the other side of this man. The one who let his guard down and overindulged in drink, laughed uncontrollably, challenged his brother-in-arms to a wrestling match, fondled a beautiful girl … the kind of man who lived dangerously sometimes. But after observing him closely for nearly a year, she doubted he did any of those things.

"Tis a lovely evening." She hugged her middle and gazed up at the star-filled sky.

"Aye," he agreed. "On a night such as this, one cannot doubt the existence of the gods. Allfather is mighty."

"Yes," she said, visually worshipping him while he focused on the heavens. "He surely is." *Especially if he made you in his image.*

Chapter Four

OLVIR WALKED THROUGH the main entrance of his father's longhouse, unprepared for the scathing reception he knew he'd get if he got caught. Most of the guards were drunk and awake, playing a game of dice at the high table with his sire. Thralls were standing at the ready with pitchers of mead, expected to refill their master's cup without him having to ask.

Hoping to go unnoticed, Olvir cringed when his father yelled his name as he reached the stairs to the loft above where he slept. "Olvir, my only useless son."

The insults were common enough before he'd left for Northumbria, but had become more frequent since his return—since his father found out he wasn't a natural fighter. "Father."

"Come here, Boy."

"I am tired."

"Is that a blatant refusal to obey your commanding officer?" his sire slurred.

Olvir rolled his eyes. "You are my father, not a captain."

"I am your blasted jarl!" Otkel slammed his massive fist on the tabletop. "Come. Drink. Roll the dice."

Knowing it futile to walk away, Olvir slowly approached the table. Fifteen bearded men regarded him.

"Hail our future lord," one of the soldiers said as he buried his face in the mouth of his drinking vessel.

"Why is there ice in your beard?" his father asked, studying him. "Has the temperature dropped that much since I last went outside to piss?" He staggered to his feet, knocking his chair over.

"No, Father." Olvir chose to get it over with. The sooner he confessed what happened, the quicker he'd be able to go to bed. "I walked home."

"In the deep snow? Where is your pony?"

Short in stature like his mother, even Olvir's two younger sisters were taller than him. A lasting embarrassment for his family. "I ride a *horse*, Father."

"If you can call that brown beast a horse."

"Call it a bloody cat if you prefer," Olvir shot back.

The soldiers laughed, waiting to see how his sire would punish his impertinence. There were always consequences when Olvir back-talked his father. Some more severe than others.

Jarl Otkel swayed and walked to where Olvir waited. He wiped his mouth with the back of his hand before he spoke. "Did you bed the wench?"

It was no secret Olvir wanted Runa. Twas the one redeeming quality his father claimed he had—extraordinary taste in women. For a match with the lady would yield many benefits for his family. "I didn't get a chance to speak with her alone."

"Why talk?" his father chided as he lewdly gyrated his hips. "There is little need for a woman's mouth, unless she uses it to…"

"I was escorted off Jarl Roald's lands," Olvir interrupted him, not needing further demonstration of how to handle a woman.

Shame filled his sire's eyes. "Escorted or forced off?"

"Depends on how you interpret it."

"Did you hear that?" The jarl gaped at his men. "My only heir is twisting the truth again to make himself look more favorable in my eyes. Only, I can see through your lies, boy. Runa deserves a real man." His father held up his thick arm. "Something she'll remember."

"Her virtue cannot be bartered for or sold to the highest bidder like a slave at market, Sir. She is a respectable lady, surrounded by family and friends, and protected by a most ardent guard."

"Oh?" Otkel seemed intrigued by that piece of information. He gestured for a thrall to bring him a wine skin. "What guard?"

"Thorolf."

"Skjold?" The jarl often relied on his highest ranking guard for answers. "Do you know the man?"

"Aye, milord." The captain stepped down from the dais. "He's known as the Giant of the North. He showed up in the Trondelag a few years ago. Little else is known about his history."

"Hmmm." His father faced him again. "Does that explain the bloody gash on your forehead?"

Shite. Olvir had tried meticulously to cover the wound with his hair. "It does."

"This *giant* dared to touch my son?"

"I'm afraid the fault is mine, Sir."

"How so?"

"After Jarl Roald introduced his children, I asked if he would submit them to baptism."

His sire's face turned a frightening shade of red before he backhanded him. "There is no room in the Trondelag for the White Christ. How many times must I tell you—demand you abandon this madness? Well? I cannot undo your conversion, Olvir. Odin rejects those who abandon him. So live with that shame behind these four walls. But when you are in public, representing me, you will not spread the foul message of

Christianity. Do you understand?"

The pain of the blow had not passed yet. In fact, his face throbbed in the spot where his father had struck him. Come morning, there'd be an angry bruise. "I refuse to hide my faith, Sir. If you are ashamed of me, send me back to Northumbria."

"You'd like that, wouldn't you?"

"Yes." No matter the situation, Olvir prided himself in always being truthful. It had earned him the name Olvir the Honest in certain circles. "Prince Ivarr would welcome me."

"Aye," his sire agreed. "Do you know how proud I was to receive a missive three months ago praising my only son's skills at reading and writing?"

Once again the guards mocked him.

"You cannot swing a sword with those undersized hands, but you can write neatly." Otkel shook his head. "Get out of my sight."

Olvir welcomed his dismissal and bowed. "Goodnight, Father."

He hurried to the narrow stairs and climbed into his modest sanctuary. He lit a candle and looked about the space. Scrolls and writing tools were strewn everywhere. Since childhood, he preferred reading over swordplay. And while his mother still lived, she encouraged him to pursue knowledge, behind his father's back.

There'd be no concealing it anymore. He intended to embrace the talents the One True God had blessed him with. And in time, once he won the heart of Runa, he'd take her back to Britain with him, where he'd never live under the weight of his sire's scorn again.

Chapter Five

ONCE THOROLF MADE sure Runa was safely inside, he bowed and returned to his seat at the high table, where his fellow captains were busy celebrating. This is where tradition left her heart regrettably divided. Though Runa valued her family, loved her country, and would just as easily give her life in defense of her home as any trained warrior, she didn't enjoy the same freedom as a man.

The only women left in the hall were thralls and whores. Wives, daughters, and sisters weren't permitted to stay after the feast ended. Roald would expect her to join the other women or to go to bed.

That's why she craved the independence associated with being a temple maiden.

A servant walked by with a tray. Runa helped herself to two servings of mead. She wasn't ready to go to bed or let Thorolf forget her. She wanted to spend more time with him, to see how he interacted with his companions.

"Give me your tray," she told the slave.

"Milady?"

"I will serve the men."

The girl stepped back, looking stunned. "The jarl will have me whipped."

Runa chuckled. "For what? Obeying me?"

The servant gave in. "Do you know how to balance it on one arm while you place the cups on the table?"

How difficult could it be? She grabbed another cup. She could outdrink half the men—a skill Konal had taught her. *Men like to get women drunk*, he'd told her years ago. *The best way to protect your virtue is to outsmart them.*

Feeling rebellious, she carried the tray to the high table and began placing the full cups in front of the men. No one noticed her and she took advantage of the opportunity to listen to what they were discussing.

"What did you do to Olvir?" one of the soldiers asked Thorolf.

"Short of cutting his bloody head off?" Thorolf took a generous swig of ale. "We talked, then he walked home."

"Talked?" Aspel questioned. "After the way you rushed over to help Lady Runa?"

"Talked," Thorolf repeated more forcefully.

"She likes you," Aspel added. "I see the way she watches you."

Thorolf released a growl, then looked sharply at his companion. "There will be no talk about the Jarl's sister."

"Then who?" Aspel pushed. "You won't touch Ingra or Mildre." He pointed across the room where the whores waited to be summoned. "No one will judge you if you slip the lady your tongue when her brother isn't looking."

Runa's cheeks burned with embarrassment. How could they talk so brazenly about her? She picked up a full cup, then glared at Aspel. "I might judge him, you animal." She poured the warm liquid over his head. "Think before you speak, Captain Aspel."

She reveled in triumph as the man pushed away from the table with his legs, his tunic and curly hair wet and sticky from the sweet drink. "Son of Odin," he cursed, shooting up from his chair. "What are you doing in the great hall, milady?"

The rest of the soldiers were laughing so hard they couldn't breathe or speak. Only Thorolf appeared unaffected. He rose, wiping his palms on his braies.

"Did you know she was standing there?" Aspel questioned him.

"Nay." Thorolf gazed at her with disapproval, then looked back at his friend. "But in the future, I suggest doing as the lady said. For the gods know all. Don't they, Lady Runa?"

"Aye," she said, feeling guilty for intruding.

Thorolf joined her on the other side of the table and whispered near her ear. "Put the tray down. I will escort you to the women's quarters."

She dispensed of the platter, but wasn't ready to retire yet. "I want to take a walk."

"Again?"

"In the open this time."

He glanced around uneasily. "Honor demands I report this incident to your brother."

"For what purpose?" She gestured at Aspel. "Hasn't he learned a hard lesson? Better than Roald could deliver with angry words or the crack of a whip?"

"Maybe."

"Do you ever compromise or admit you're wrong, Captain Thorolf?"

"I've never misjudged anyone."

"No?" She blinked rapidly. "Agree there is more than one solution for a problem."

"I believe in right and wrong, milady. That's the philosophy I live by. And it has served me well."

She couldn't fault him for having high moral standards. "Very well." She'd let him keep his rules for another night.

"About the walk..."

"Come. I will take you."

She wanted to explore the woods near the river, a place she often visited after dark as a child. Spirits wandered in the forest during the winter, looking for a way to rejoin their loved ones in the afterlife.

She walked briskly to the footpath.

"Where are you going?" Thorolf asked.

"This way," she said, not stopping.

"What kind of answer is that?" He touched her arm from behind. "Why do you resist?"

She wheeled about, facing him. "What do you mean?"

"I'm a quiet man, Runa," he started. "But I take everything in. You are unsettled."

"I am unhappy."

He tilted his head. "The world is at your feet. You have but to choose a fate."

"Spoken like a true warrior who knows nothing about women."

"I know enough," he countered.

"Do you? Then perhaps you understand my plight, Sir. For as the only daughter of Jarl Brandr, I am expected to marry a man my brother approves of, providing my family with wealth, lands, and a new ally. That is the extent of my fate, Captain."

"I'm sorry."

"As am I, for my dream will remain just that."

A spell of silence followed before he caressed her cheek with his thumb. She closed her eyes, relishing in his touch, knowing his motivation for doing it was simply to comfort her. But in her mind—in her deepest fantasy ... it could never be. Brief as the tender moment was, it meant more to Runa than anything he could have said.

"What dream do you wish to live?"

"If I speak it, you'll laugh at me."

"Never."

Could she trust him with such an intimate secret? Only her family and maids knew. "I wish to serve as a temple maiden."

"What shame in such a noble calling, Lady?"

She averted her teary gaze. "Our zealous jarl would disagree."

"I will not speak against him."

"I'd expect no less from an honorable man as you, Captain Thorolf. You are a better person than I am. For I do not love my eldest brother as I should or my dearly departed father. Too much has happened between us—too many harsh words spoken—too many regrets."

"Time will change your mind."

"Because I'm a woman?"

"Partly," he said. "The rest involves the faith you have in the gods. Anyone willing to forego a life of privilege in order to serve Allfather is blessed with humility and wisdom. Open your heart to Odin, Runa, he will comfort you in your darkest hour."

"Even when I am forced to take vows with a man I do not love?"

She already owed Thorolf a great debt for protecting her tonight. Burdening him with more problems didn't seem right, but how could she fight against what came so naturally? She trusted him implicitly. The physical attraction remained only a sliver of what she felt in his presence.

She wiped her eyes, then smiled up at him. "We've forgotten the point of our outing, Sir."

"Aye." He offered his arm. "You wanted to walk through the woods?"

"Yes," she said. "As long as you stay with me."

Chapter Six

"THE GIRL HAS gone too far this time," Jarl Roald addressed his wife as he paced the length of their bedchamber. "She threatened a man with a knife, Eva."

"And you witnessed all this while drinking your fill of mead and introducing your son to hundreds of guests?"

"I know what I saw."

Eva repositioned herself on the bed. "Words wasted on a woman like me, Sir. For you know in my world nothing can be taken at face value. A person's motivation is more important. Did you ask her why she got so angry at Olvir? Hasn't he been absent for years, only just returned?"

"Aye." Roald scrubbed his face. "All the more reason to be accommodating. Even if the man is as irritating as a pack of old women. My reputation is at stake, not Runa's. My children won't be shamed by her."

"*Our* children."

"Our children," he repeated, yielding to his lovely wife. "She's unstable. Selfish. Determined to get her way."

Eva chuckled then, drawing his questioning gaze. "A description that fits nearly every member of your family."

"Does it now?"

"Perfectly. The only reason it troubles you so deeply is because she's female. If Konal or Haakon did the same, would you be here now, complaining?"

He frowned. "A wife should support her husband."

"No," she disagreed. "A wife should guide her husband back to the right path if he's lost his way. Remember our promise, Roald?"

"Yes," he admitted. "To always tell the truth to each other."

"Aye. Runa is a spirited girl with dreams of her own. The very thing you admired me for."

"That is different."

"Oh?"

"You aren't the daughter of a jarl."

"No, I am not. But a birthright doesn't change a person's heart."

"Maybe not," he said. "But it makes her beholden to something greater than herself. Something more important than me."

"The gods? For that's the only thing I can think of that's more important than my loving husband. And Runa wishes to serve the gods alone."

Roald growled, angered by the mere mention of his sister's desire to be a temple maiden. "She's been talking about it again?"

"No. I inquired about it the other day. Her happiness is a priority."

"You have no time to worry about her." He walked to the side of the bed and kissed the top of her head. "You need to rest and get your strength back so our son and daughter can benefit from their mother's love and care."

"I am well, Roald, more than ready to resume my role in this household."

"You lost too much blood giving birth, Eva." He squeezed her hand. "I won't risk your life."

"Be gentle with the girl. She's been through so much this

year. Your father's death, Konal and Silvia's surprise marriage, and our union. You spend so much time lecturing her on what she's expected to do, but all she sees is her elder brothers breaking with tradition and marrying women your sire would have never approved of. Don't you think this kind of behavior inspires rebellion rather than discipline?"

He gazed upon his wife with deep respect, knowing she spoke truthfully. Yes, his actions were a negative influence on Runa. However, when it came to his sister's future, he swore to carry out his father's wishes. The girl must marry. Soon. "I will speak with her."

"You'll be patient?"

"If she is forthcoming and reasonable."

Eva rewarded him with a smile, then curled up on her side, still tired from the long delivery of their beloved twins. Roald closed the door quietly, sincerely happy for the first time in his life. He walked through the great hall, headed for the women's quarters on the other side of the longhouse.

He knocked on Runa's chamber door.

"Enter," she called.

He found her seated at a table, reading a scroll. "Are you too busy to speak with me?"

Runa quickly rolled the parchment up. "I am never too busy for my jarl." She stood then, motioning to an empty chair. "Join me, Brother?"

He did. "I want a full account of what transpired between you and Olvir last night."

Runa sighed. "Did you not hear his words, Sir? He dared to ask you to submit my nephew and niece to baptism. Those words alone are reason enough to take his life."

Roald swallowed his laughter, secretly admiring her fierceness. But her aggressive behavior couldn't go unpunished. The eyes of every woman in the crowd had been upon her, watching closely. Runa must live according to the traditions of her family, serving as a role model for all the impressionable young girls dependent on his family for sustenance.

"That isn't a satisfactory answer."

She waved her hands. "What do you want me to say? I was born with the same temperament as you. When I see or hear something that goes against everything I believe in..."

"You are a woman."

"I am Norse."

"You will learn to manage that quick temper and sharp tongue or I will be forced to take action."

She thrust her hand on her hip, throwing him a challenging look. "And what will you do? Take a strap to my back the way Father did? Withhold food? Confine me to my room?"

Roald stood. "I'll marry you off to the most decrepit suitor I can find from the furthest reaches in the south where belief in the White Christ is taking root. And if you think my demands are too much, Runa, wait until you find out how strict Christian priests are with females. They blame a woman for the downfall of humanity."

She clicked her tongue. "I'll resist you."

"I would expect no less."

"I will take a public oath, Roald. I will swear allegiance to Odin and make it impossible for you to deny my true calling."

He captured her arm from across the table and gave her a shake. "Empty threats. Konal's future is still dependent upon your obedience, Runa. Did you think the fate-binding held no weight? We are at peace now, but if I deny Konal's right to establish his own steading, he will leave Norway. Is that what you want, Girl?"

She yanked her arm free. "What did I do to earn your bitterness?"

"I made a promise, Runa. Now that I have my own family to think of, I refuse to risk their future by breaking my oath to Father just to appease a girl's mindless dream of being a temple maiden. If I fail to honor my sire's dying wishes, the gods will penalize me."

"I've never known you to fear anything, not even the gods."

"I've never been jarl before. And it's not fear, Runa. Don't mistake honor for fear. Cooperate and I will give you a say in what man you marry. Defy me and I alone will choose."

She sucked in a ragged breath. "This is my punishment for defending our family?"

"You threatened the son of a jarl. His words were ill spoken, but he made a fool of himself without your interference. Olvir is a weakling, Runa. No one took him seriously but you. My captains are tasked with guarding the great hall. You owe Thorolf much for taking charge of the situation when he did. For if that blade had drawn even a drop of Olvir's blood, his father would have come here demanding a fight or weregild to reclaim his family's honor."

"I care little for your politics, Brother."

"Aye," he said. "All the more reason for you to keep your mouth shut in public. Carelessness like yours start wars."

"And your disregard destroys families."

Roald stalked to the door, irritated by her continued unruliness. "You will present yourself at the eventide meal as a lady. Dressed appropriately with a smile on your pretty face. You will eat and drink in silence unless you have something useful to say. Do you understand?"

"Aye," she said, fisting her hands at her sides. Someday she'd walk away from Roald for the last time, never to look back, happy to be rid of him forever.

Chapter Seven

THOROLF STARED AT the empty seat only three places down from his own spot at the high table. A second trestle had been added to the dais to accommodate the jarl's growing family. Roald, Eva, Konal, Silvia, Haakon, the chair kept open for the absent brother, Bruin, and Runa were supposed to be in attendance at every eventide meal, as were the jarl's four captains. But tonight, Runa had ignored the order her brother had given her earlier.

Several influential men were in attendance, invited to meet the jarl's beautiful sister. Thorolf fisted his hands under the table as he chewed on a mouthful of venison and then swallowed it. Roald had secretly assigned him to keep watch over Runa. A responsibility he took very seriously but should have passed on. He couldn't possibly remain neutral with Runa. He cared about her and admired her unadulterated passion and devotion for the gods.

Not to mention the assortment of jarls and first sons waiting eagerly to lay eyes on the promised girl. Thorolf's gaze moved slowly over the men who were stuffing their faces with the jarl's bounty. Seated at the next table, they were dressed in finery and attended by their own thralls.

Thorolf knew five of them. The first, Jarl Durin, ruled a small but prosperous area to the east. Hedin and Lodmund were the sons of jarls. Jarl Vandrad hailed from the southern regions. And Axel was a Swedish prince—the worthiest suitor of all. But the dark-haired stranger at the end of the table bothered him the most. He had the eyes of a ravenous wolf and wore Saxon armor to eat in. Did the stranger wear it to bed, too?

"Where is your mind?"

Thorolf twisted in his chair as soon as he heard Roald's deep voice. The jarl was sitting next to him now.

"Too much wine, my lord," he lied, wiping his mouth dry with the back of his hand.

Roald slapped his back. "Only the best drink for our honored guests. But these great men won't stay long if my sister doesn't do her duty. Bring her here, Thorolf, even if you have to throw her over your shoulder kicking and screaming. Better a potential suitor sees Runa at her worst now than send her back weeks after the wedding night with a complaint about her rebellious nature."

Thorolf left the great hall, determined to escort Runa to the feast willingly. He'd never laid hands upon a woman in an aggressive manner. Unless wrestling with childhood friends counted. That memory made him smile as he stepped into the passageway that led to the women's quarters. He was greeted by several thralls as he passed by.

"Where is Lady Runa?" he asked one.

"In her chamber," the girl pointed.

He nodded and didn't hesitate to open the door without knocking first. Let Runa taste the urgency of the situation here instead of making a public spectacle of herself.

"Captain Thorolf," the girl greeted him nonchalantly as her maid worked on her pitch-colored hair. "Is something wrong?"

Ragnarok couldn't shake this woman's resolve.

"Jarl Roald..."

"Yes, yes," she tsked. "Let me guess. My impatient brother has sent you to fetch me because I'm a few minutes late for the feast?"

"Aye."

Her soft, feminine laughter warmed his insides.

"Doesn't he know I wish to look my best before he opens the bids for my betrothal?" The maid finished with her hair and stepped back, offering Runa a flat, polished disc of bronze so she could admire herself. "Yes, I think I'm ready. Do you agree, Captain?"

Unable to resist looking, Thorolf studied her features appreciatively. Her hair had been pulled away from her face, intricately braided at the sides, its length twisted high on her head and pinned in place. She had a long, elegant neck and broad shoulders for a woman. A gold, Thor's hammer pendant hung from the chain about her throat.

Somehow, Thorolf always found his gaze drawn to her almond-shaped eyes. At the moment, they were bright with mischief.

"Well, Sir?"

He cleared his throat. He'd almost forgotten about her gown, the color matched the deep green of her eyes, revealed just a hint of her milk-white flesh at the breast, and perfectly complimented her slim waist and full hips. "If your aim is to snare a husband, Lady, you have my word, you won't fail."

She chuckled again. "Am I mistaken, Captain, or was that a compliment?"

"Aye." He sighed. "But you don't need my praise. That glass you just peered into should give you the answers you seek."

"A special gift from my brother, Bruin, after he returned from Baghdad years ago. Though it gives me a chance to see myself, only a man's opinion counts on such a matter. My self-perception is not the concern of my brother. Only what others think of me."

The girl intended to bait him into saying something against Jarl Roald. But his loyalty was unshakeable. She'd have to do better than that. "Our jarl wishes to secure a good future for you, Lady. To entrust your life to a man worthy of your respect and love. What if he didn't care so much? What if he chose a man of poor character? One who would neglect you and beat you into submission?"

Runa snorted. "I'd die before I'd let a man hit me."

"Precisely my point. Cooperate with your brother. Give him a chance to forge an alliance with one of these men that will both benefit you and your family."

"I want to be a temple maiden, not a wife."

"Shhh." Thorolf surged forward and covered her mouth with two fingers. "These walls have eyes and ears."

She shrugged. "As do the trees and river. For anything I say is instantly reported to my brother." She gave him an accusing look.

"Not by my lips. I swear it."

"I believe you. And as I've said many times, you are the most honorable man in the Trondelag, perhaps in the world over."

Thorolf didn't want to be known for that alone, not to a woman like Runa. If only he could temporarily break his oath to the jarl and give this girl a taste of the fire that burned within him—speak the words that filled his heart and mind. Share his deepest feelings, the ones best expressed in a bed in the middle of the night.

"It pleases me that you trust me. Will you let me escort you to the great hall now?"

"Tell me of the men, first … the dark one my maids do not

recognize. Is he as wild looking as they say?"

Thorolf took a restless stance. He didn't want to discuss her suitors in detail. Truth be told, he disliked each one for different reasons, thoughts of which he'd keep to himself. The dark stranger bothered him the most. "He wears foreign armor, a cloak trimmed with fur, and a black tunic. I know nothing of his background or family. He hasn't spoken with the other guests."

Runa folded her hands over her stomach, looking surprised. "You observed him that closely?"

"Tis my way, Lady Runa."

"Yes."

Thorolf offered his arm then, hoping Runa would go quietly. Much to his relief, she did.

They walked down the corridor together, then entered the great hall where entertainers were playing a song on their flutes and rebecs. The music stopped as soon as Jarl Roald stood. "Beloved Sister," he said sarcastically. "I am happy to see you. I thought you were lost to us."

Laughter sounded as Thorolf walked to the high table, deposited Runa in her seat, and then claimed his own.

Roald stared at his sister for a long moment, then raised his cup. "A toast to my beautiful sister. May the gods grant her long life and happiness."

The crowd cheered.

"And a strong back," the dark-haired stranger Runa had questioned Thorolf about called out before he took a drink.

Thorolf shot up from his chair and unsheathed his weapon, offended by what the man suggested.

"Wait." Jarl Roald signaled him to stand down. "Explain the meaning of your words, Jarl Skrymir, before my captain challenges you to a fight."

Skrymir glanced casually at Thorolf, appearing more humored than worried. "I didn't think I needed to explain. Are we here to judge the lady for her fitness as a wife or saint? My meaning is clear. A strong back for bearing the brunt of my weight as I climb on top of her in the wedding bed."

Thorolf growled as he heard the snickers following the crude comment.

"Have you forgotten where you are?" Roald set his cup aside, rounded the table, then stepped off the dais.

Skrymir stood. "In your hallowed hall, Jarl Roald. And I've shown nothing but respect for your family. My men warned you about the kind of man I am. I live in the far north, not here among the pampered and civilized people in the lowlands. If your sister possessed a horse face, I would not have been inspired to say such a thing. But look at her—her beauty is rivaled by few women I've seen. What else is a man supposed to think about? I need a wife and heir. You require new alliances to expand your power."

"Aye, I do." Roald stopped in front of Skrymir's table, Thorold standing behind him. "I suggest learning to hold your tongue. We do not say such things about our women, not in mixed company, and surely not in the great hall."

The stranger nodded and reached inside his cloak, revealing a leather coin bag. He dropped it on the table. "Recompense for my bad manners."

Roald picked up the bag and weighed it in his palm. "An acceptable apology."

"Meant for the lady," Skrymir looked over Roald's shoulder.

"Runa," Roald called. "Join us."

Thorolf closed his eyes, itching to strike the bastard with a fist. But Jarl Roald had made peace with him. Thorolf opened his eyes then, sheathed his weapon, and relaxed as best he could under the circumstances.

Runa appeared at her brother's side.

"Runa, meet Jarl Skrymir. He has traveled many days to be here," Roald introduced her.

She curtsied. "Where do you come from, Sir?"

"Beyond the lands of the Laplanders, where the sun sets for months at a time in the winter and blazes gloriously for months in the summer."

"The dark reaches," Runa commented. "Where men and beasts live as one."

"Aye."

Runa gazed at her brother. "Mother used to tell me stories about these men. How brutal and dangerous they are. You'd send me there?"

Roald blinked several times but didn't answer her. "This is a gift from Jarl Skrymir." He offered her the coins.

"Your words did not escape me, Jarl Skrymir. In the Trondelag, women are judged for more than their physical strength. It takes a strong back to cultivate extensive gardens, to cook in the kitchens, to carry children about all day while we work. I've managed the store rooms, livestock, smoke houses, tended to the needs of my family and thralls, overseen the weaving room, dealt with greater men than you, and still found the desire to smile every night at the eventide meal. Passing an unmemorable night with you in your bedchamber would be nothing compared to what I now do."

She made sure to smile demurely before she finished her thought. "And though I am not the kind of woman to turn down coin when it's so hard to come by in these days of great turmoil, I must refuse your gift. Please donate it to the less fortunate, or better yet, to the temple maidens who pray for boorish men like you every day."

Roald's eyes narrowed and his mouth dropped open.

"The lady has a charitable heart," Skrymir observed. "You will make a good mother."

"No," Runa disagreed. "I will make a fine temple maiden." She stormed off, leaving a furious brother and shocked suitor behind.

"Thorolf," his lord spoke through gritted teeth. "Take my sister to Odin's altar and make her sacrifice a bird or two in atonement for her continued disobedience and rude behavior toward our guest."

"Aye." Thorolf, once again, left the great hall in search of the lady he was sure no man could tame or hold back for too long.

Chapter Eight

RUNA HAD LIED to everyone for the sake of her pride. Jarl Skrymir's words had, indeed, cut deep, leaving her both disgusted and disappointed in Roald. How could her brother allow such a brute to sit at the same table with honorable men? To step inside their father's house? To make an offer of marriage for her? She absolutely refused to defile her family's name by considering such a match. The man wasn't good enough to share space with the horses in the stable.

Feeling trapped, she left the longhouse by the back door, breathing in the crisp nighttime air. As always, soldiers were gathered around the eventide fires, drinking and eating, playing dice or cards, and discussing their latest conquests. Idle talk as far as she was concerned.

A couple grunted at her as she passed by, paying no heed to a lone girl walking about. She had grabbed a cloak off a peg by the entrance, hoping to conceal her gown and richly adorned hair. For no warrior would let the jarl's sister go unescorted.

Runa had been known to dress in the rags of a thrall to gain freedom from watchful eyes. She'd even donned a slave collar before. Peace and quiet were her favorite companions—whether found by the river or in the woods. There, she could think clearly and pray uninhibited, pleading her cause to Allfather and Thor.

Tonight, her aim was the forest, to the white stone altar where generations of her kinswomen had made blood sacrifices to the gods in search of answers. Cages containing birds and rabbits were kept nearby so anyone in need could fulfill their sacrificial duty. Unlike the White Christ, Viking gods required fresh blood to intervene on the behalf of a mortal.

More than anyone, Runa needed help, desperately. If her eldest brother had his way, she'd be married by tomorrow and sent away. Away from the place she loved and everyone she knew. Marriage didn't excite her the way it did other women. Oh, she appreciated the idea of joining with a man. It must be special, for why else would a temple maiden be forbidden to have sex? Everybody must sacrifice something to serve Odin.

She arrived at the clearing where the altar stood. Bonfires were lit nightly and watched over by two priests who lived in a cottage in the woods. Ringed by ancient trees, the space had been carefully planned long before the main longhouse had ever been built. Wherever she stood, moonlight hit her and illuminated the sacred clearing in silvery light. She gazed skyward then, admiring the stars and thin veil of clouds. Inches of snow covered the ground, but the holy men and their servants labored each day to clear as much of it as possible.

"Hear me, great Odin. I am but a mere girl. Prisoner in my brother's house. A thrall possesses more freedom than I. For I am expected to choose a husband from among the men sitting in the great hall. All of them fall short of my favor." She wiped a single tear from her eye, overcome with emotion suddenly. "I do not wish to leave the Trondelag for a man. I wish to leave by own accord—to travel northward to the shadowlands where your temple sits. Where my unknown sisters wait for me in the shelter of your holy place. Where I can see and hear you daily. Where men do not interfere with life. Where I can call upon your name and know my privacy will be respected."

There was so much more to say tonight. Heart full of feelings and her mind filled with unspoken words, she hoped for a sign from her beloved god.

"I am not a dreamer as my brother claims. My thoughts are rooted in reality. I seek no wealth or comfort beyond what I need to sustain me. Though I adore children, I have never desired to give birth. To marry. To serve a man when I can serve you." She dropped to her knees, still steps away from the altar stone. "Roald is my jarl. I am bound by blood and honor to obey him. But he doesn't take my feelings to heart. I am but an empty vessel to him, born to advance his holdings, to secure an alliance with another family. Am I selfish or wrong to seek a way closer to you, Allfather?"

She paused, waiting to hear if the wind carried Odin's voice as it had once a long time ago. At six, she'd heard the god's voice while she sat in the center of the clearing one night alone. Before she could answer, one of her sire's captains had snatched her up and taken her back to the women's quarters, leaving a hole in her heart.

Perhaps that moment had determined her fate—turned her into the restless girl she'd grown up to be. Shaped her into a woman who had little regard for tradition and family responsibilities. More important things existed in the world. The sanctity of the gods was being challenged, a new faith from across the North Sea had invaded the southern reaches of her country recently. And bloody battles were being waged to resist the White Christ. She wanted to do her part to protect the old ways, to safeguard her own faith.

"Roald fate-binded me to my brother, Konal, as a means to control me. Reveal to me how I can break this curse."

She rose to her feet, then walked the short distance to the

altar. The nearest cage held three chickens, near frozen from the cold. Though she preferred the blood of wild birds over domesticated ones, she'd do what she had to. As she reached for the latch on the wire door, she heard a twig snap.

"Lady Runa," Thorolf called.

She closed her eyes and cursed under her breath. Why did this man appear at the times he did? And why did her heart skip a beat whenever he said her name? Did she even need to ask? She turned around, finding him in the clearing.

The captain had jumped into action to defend her honor after Jarl Skrymir had insulted her. For that, she, once again, owed him endless gratitude. But this time, he was intruding. "What are you doing here, Captain?"

"Protecting you."

"From what?" she asked. "Moonlight?"

He shook his head and came closer. "From many things, Lady. Including men who deserve to die."

She watched him closely, appreciative of his presence. Did the man even know how handsome he was? Did he know other men feared him? Not just for his hulking frame, but the way he carried himself—silent and deadly—formidable in every way she could think of.

"You want to cut the jarl's head off his shoulders?"

"Aye, I do. And feed his liver to the ravens. Think what kind of answer his entrails would get you from the gods."

She couldn't resist laughing. "Perhaps we could join forces after Skrymir has gone to bed." Only a couple feet from her now, she could see the intensity in Thorolf's eyes, could actually feel it, like heat coming off a fire.

"A fantasy," he commented.

"A good one."

"Aye."

"Did my brother send you?"

"Yes. But I would have come anyway."

She rubbed the nervous sweat from her palms on her cloak. "What will happen after I'm married and no longer have someone like you to keep me out of trouble?"

"Do you mean what you say to Allfather?"

Her shoulders drooped then, for her words were meant for the gods alone. Someone might think her mad for speaking as freely as she did—for saying what she dared say. "I do."

"I-I..."

She'd never heard the captain stutter before. "What is it?" she asked, concerned.

"I am humbled, lady. Truly. If I could change your brother's mind, I would."

"Thank you, Captain. My sister-in-law has tried to reason with Roald, too. I've begged and argued with him, to no avail. He is determined to carry out my sire's wishes. You and I know dead men have no power in Midgard. Even from Valhalla, all Father can do is watch over us."

"Surely you understand the importance of a dying man's wishes. Especially if Jarl Roald swore an oath. Men live by different standards than women, are expected to do certain things without fail."

Runa crossed her arms over her chest, not liking his last words. "I am less a person because I do not have a ..."

"Never," he cut her off, obviously anticipating what she was going to say. "Not less a person, just different."

"Yes. Decidedly so, Captain."

"I have offended you."

"Nay. I am disappointed. You often think as I do, or at least agree with what I say. So when you don't, it bothers me. Sometimes I think you come from a different place, another world even." She gestured at the stars.

"What world?" He followed her gaze.

"Asgard?"

"You see me as a god?" He puffed his chest out. "I will remember that in the future."

She chuckled. "Perhaps Jotunheim is a better fit for you, Thorolf."

He laughed. "I am no giant."

"But you are," she argued, once again staring at him for too long, her admiration never hidden. "Or maybe you're from one of those blazing stars. A place no man has ever heard of."

"I like to see you smile. To hear your laughter."

She sighed. "It seems this happy moment must come to an abrupt end." She searched his face for any sign that she might be wrong, but Thorolf's expression sobered. "My brother demands my return to apologize to our guests."

"No," he said. "In fact, I'm sure our lord would rather you stay away. However, I am here to make sure you atone for your misdeeds by offering a sacrifice to Odin."

"My brother doesn't have that right."

"Why, Lady? Why do you struggle so hard, make life more difficult than it need be? There are ways to pacify men, even one as rigid as Jarl Roald."

"And you're going to instruct me on how to please my brother? How to deceive him?"

He shook his head. "Never to deceive."

"Yes," she said. "I must take care to choose my words more precisely when speaking with you, Captain."

"The men your brother has selected as possible husbands are going to be here for days. Try to get to know them. I can answer whatever questions you have about one or all, with the exception of the dark bastard."

"This will ease the tension between Roald and me?"

"There's more if you're willing to listen."

"Aye."

"You have no choice but to pick a husband. Once you've selected one, ask your brother to grant you some time to visit where this suitor lives, to get to know his family, to see how he treats his people. I will do whatever I can to help you in this cause, including advising Jarl Roald to grant you this small request. If you find the man unsuitable once you've gotten to know him, return home. It is not a perfect solution, Lady, but it gives you time to adapt to your new circumstances."

"And quite possibly prevent me from marrying the wrong man."

"Aye. Jarl Roald will assign several guards to accompany you, too. I will make sure to be among them."

Runa wet her lips. *Why?* lingered in her mind. The same question that always dominated her thoughts whenever Thorolf was involved with her. Why would he do this? Why was he always willing to help her? Why did he care a fig for where she ended up? Why did he always look like he was staring right through her? Better yet, staring into the depths of her being…

She kept those intimate inquiries to herself, though. The captain had already done more than expected. "I will think this over."

"I am glad to hear it." He walked around her, stooped down in front of the cage, opened it, then grabbed one of the chickens by the neck. "Time to uphold your brother's command."

Yes—she'd do that at least.

Thorolf wrung the bird's neck, the most merciful way to sacrifice an animal. Then he laid the creature over the flat altar stone and unsheathed his long knife and gave it to her.

She moved closer to the altar. "Hear me, great Odin…"

Murmuring a more customary chant this time, Runa fulfilled her obligation to Roald. She'd not give her brother any reason to doubt Thorolf's devotion. With one sure cut, she shed the necessary blood to attain absolution from the gods for her supposed disobedience.

Chapter Nine

TWO DAYS LATER, Thorolf found himself the unfortunate victim of his own advice to Runa. She'd chosen one of her suitors to spend time with and now the captain acted as their chaperone, shadowing her and Prince Axel on an afternoon walk.

The prince fingered a strand of Runa's long hair. "Tis as soft as a flower petal," he said.

Thorolf rolled his eyes, wishing he was at the practice field with the other soldiers instead of overhearing lovespeak that made him want to punch a tree, or even the prince himself.

"Thank you," Runa whispered, batting her eyelashes like a mindless girl.

Thorolf hadn't imagined Runa would embrace the role of the obedient sister so enthusiastically. Or that she'd welcome the admiration of one of her suitors so easily. Regardless, Jarl Roald welcomed the sudden change in her behavior and even thanked Thorolf for setting his sister on the right path.

The sooner my sister is wed and away from the Trondelag, the sooner we can focus on the political benefits from her union, the jarl had told him only yesterday.

Runa hadn't exaggerated about her brother's motivations for finding her a husband. It pained Thorolf to think his lord didn't realize her full potential. How her talents might be wasted on a man who didn't understand or deserve her. The captain did, however—completely. And though his hands were tied when it came to interfering on her marriage plans, the one thing he could do, would do, was to see her happy and safe. His sword was pledged to protect her from harm. And if that meant flaying a prince, so be it.

"I am aware of your love for the gods," Axel said. "There is a family altar near my home. The stones were transported from my birthplace."

"All the way from Sweden?"

"Aye," he said.

"How did you come to live in Norway? Why are you not with your family?"

The prince stopped walking. "I have six brothers and eight sisters," he explained. "The island of Gotland isn't large enough to support all of us. My father has struggled to distribute our inheritances fairly. But I am the third son. When my sire offered to give me his lands here, I gladly accepted."

"Fifteen children?" Runa asked. "Your mother gave birth fifteen times?"

Axel chuckled at her shocked expression. "Aye."

"Is she still..."

"Alive and well," Axel assured her. "Though she is no longer breeding."

"Praise Odin for that." Runa covered her mouth then. "I am sorry, Prince Axel. I have a bad habit of speaking my mind without thinking about what I say first."

Again, the good natured prince smiled. "Tis one of the things I like most about you. Rest assured you need not fear for your health, Lady Runa. If I am fortunate enough to be chosen as your husband, I wouldn't expect you to have so many children. Six or seven would please me fine."

Thorolf waited for Runa to say something—to reject the prince's dream of such a large family. But she didn't speak, only stared northward, in the direction the footpath followed.

"Of course, I would like a son or two," Axel continued. "But I favor my nieces over most of my nephews. So I'd be equally happy with daughters."

"How many nieces and nephews do you have?" Runa queried.

"Fourteen."

"Your parents must be overjoyed by so many grandchildren."

"Aye."

"As you know, I have two nephews and one niece. I adore all three."

They wandered a bit further up the trail.

"You have been very kind to me, Sir." Runa addressed the prince. "If it pleases you, I'd like to visit your home before I make a decision about who I want to marry."

"Please me?" Axel cradled her hands between his. "I'd consider it an honor. You understand it is far north from here? It would take a week of steady travel. But I promise you, the landscape rivals the beauty of the Trondelag. Wildflowers as far as the eye can see—peaks twice as soaring as the ones about us now. My longhouse is situated between two fjords. I own thirty ships, Lady Runa. A fleet fit for a king. Enough vessels to aid your brother if ever he is attacked by his enemies. Enough men to lay ruin to any rival."

Thorolf didn't like where the conversation was going. Prince Axel possessed wealth and power. Many thought highly of the man—he had a reputation for being fair with his people. But when it came to protecting his holdings, to defending his family's honor, Axel had earned a name for himself in Norway—

The Golden Avenger.

The captain silently scrutinized the prince, taking in his light hair and icy eyes. Royal blood flowed through his veins. If Runa chose him, their children would be princes and princesses. And she … the captain looked at Runa then. She, too, would be a princess.

"Let us not waste any more time," Axel said. "I will speak with Jarl Roald tonight."

"Aye," Runa agreed, allowing the prince to hold her hand as they headed back to the longhouse.

"SHE HAS OUTWITTED me this time," Jarl Roald complained as he paced the length of his solar. "Where did she get the idea to *visit* Prince Axel's home? How did she even know to ask?"

Thorolf wouldn't volunteer any information unless his lord asked him directly.

"The worst of it is I am obligated to say yes. If I don't, I risk offending the man I want most for an ally." Roald stared at Thorolf. "Have you nothing to say about it?"

"I will accompany her, of course."

"Yes." The jarl rubbed his chin. "You seem to share a close relationship with my sister. She obviously trusts you—feels comfortable enough to confide in you."

"Aye."

"And did she give you any warning about this?"

"No, milord."

"Did she visit my wife or Silvia recently?"

"Nay."

"The spaewife?"

"No."

"Perhaps Konal? He'd counsel her this way—help her avoid

getting married for as long as she could."

"With the exception of being abed, Runa has never been out of my sight."

"I am left with no choice. Inform my sister that her request is granted. Pick three other guards you trust to escort Runa and Prince Axel to his home. I expect regular reports, Captain Thorolf. Fair warning, your journey will take you very near Odin's temple, a place I know my sister longs to visit. Under no circumstances is she to be allowed to go there. And if you value my opinion, when you come within a hundred miles of the place and make camp, tie her to the closest tree. For I have no doubt she'll try to run away or manipulate the prince into stopping there."

Feeling much like a length of rope being tugged from both ends, Thorolf knew he needed to settle things with the jarl before he left the Trondelag. "Do I have your permission to speak freely?"

Roald poured himself a measure of mead and gulped it down, then offered Thorolf a drink. "Don't we have an understanding, Thorolf?"

"Aye." The captain accepted the cup and drank his fill.

"The reason I value you so much—entrusted you with the honor of guarding my family—is because I know you speak only truth. You need not seek my permission whenever you have something to say."

"If I am to serve your sister without fail, I need you to release me from my oath to you."

Roald frowned. "Why?"

"A man cannot serve two masters."

"Runa is no master, she's a woman."

Jarl Roald's marriage to his Sami wife, Eva, had changed him for the better. But occasionally, the captain felt he was talking to

Roald's dead father, Jarl Brandr. A man who felt women should remain silent and had no say in their futures. Thorolf wished Roald trusted his sister more. But in the scheme of things, the fact he'd given her a choice in who she married, suggested Roald cared for her, though he'd never admit it.

"I must insist," Thorolf said. "It is tradition where I come from."

"Yes," Roald mumbled. "I often forget the men of Borg are different than most. You spent too much time in the frigid crosswinds when you were a boy, Captain. It has muddled your mind, I think."

Thorolf chuckled. "My mother saw fit to keep my ears covered as a boy," he said. "I am of sound mind."

Roald sat on the chair at his table. "I trust you. But someday, Captain, I will inquire about you to the chieftain in Borg. You've been in my service so long; I never saw reason to question your credentials as a soldier. Over time, you've earned the admiration of my family and men. A rare accomplishment."

Thorolf bowed, accepting the praise with confidence. He served without fail. As his father and brothers had before him. But the captain had never uttered their names or even his mother's name. For all were dead. Instead, he chose to invest his time and energy in serving a family similar to his own. It eased his pain and suffering, gave him a reason to want to live.

"I am honored to know you."

Roald carved something into a piece of deer skin with his knife, then handed it to Thorolf. "Here is your temporary reprieve from allegiance to me."

He gazed at the runic symbol representing defense of someone he loved and respected. It meant nothing to anyone else, but to Thorolf, it represented everything he believed in. Free now to focus solely on Runa, anything he said to her or did for her from this point forward, could be kept between them. He no longer answered to Jarl Roald first. He tucked the scrap in his belt.

"Thank you."

Roald waved his hand dismissively. "It is I who should thank you. Runa is a great burden to any man. Though I am pleased she's interested in Prince Axel, I suspect she has ulterior motives. Axel is a fierce warrior, but he's never loved a woman. That inexperience will cost him dearly when dealing with a girl as unpredictable as my sister."

"Or keep him pleasantly entertained."

"Yes." Roald laughed. "Odin save the man who ever truly loves her."

Chapter Ten

JARL ROALD STOOD at a distance watching while Prince Axel's retinue of soldiers and thralls rushed to finish packing the horses for the journey home. Against his better judgment, Roald had given permission for Runa to leave the Trondelag, unwed and in the care of Thorolf and her maid, Auda. Though everything appeared normal at the surface, dark thoughts plagued the jarl's mind. And something even more troublesome soured his gut.

"You must learn to let go." Eva slipped her arms around his waist from behind, resting her sweet face against his back. She gave him an extra tight squeeze. "She is a good girl, Roald. As independent as her brothers, but also as honorable."

"As long as it serves her purpose." He turned around and tugged his wife into his arms.

Eva gazed up at him. "A terrible thing to say about your only sister."

"Experience has taught me well, Eva. One should listen when an old dog barks. And no matter how hard I try to clear my mind, I can hear my father's voice warning me to put an end to this deception."

Eva stepped back. "Deception? Did you not demand Runa choose a husband from among the men you invited here? Threatened to marry her off to a beast of your choice if she didn't? Do you blame her for selecting the wealthiest and most handsome of the five? The one you prayed she'd have the sense to choose. Visiting where she might call home one day is a prudent decision. She deserves to see how the prince conducts himself at home. Whether his even temperament is genuine or not."

Roald nodded in agreement, though reluctantly. "I gave *you* no choice."

"Wrong." Eva slapped his chest playfully. "I let you think you were in control, Husband."

"Did you now?" He kissed her tenderly. "I am not the one who donned a veil and snuck into the jarl's chamber late at night to seduce him. It seems you couldn't resist my masculine charms. So if we look at this rationally, I'd say I was in control the whole time."

"Even so," Eva said, "Runa's life is taking a different path than ours. Let her enjoy her maidenhood while she can. Soon enough, she'll be joined at the hip to a man and children. Let Prince Axel spoil her—woo her properly. And if she accepts him, think of the celebration we'll have."

Roald pulled on the end of his beard, mulling over his wife's words. Yes, if Runa accepted the prince's troth, then he'd rejoice at gaining such a powerful brother-in-law. But if the girl rebelled as she often did, he'd punish her severely for humiliating him. "I will try. Perhaps Odin spoke to her—showed her how unreasonable she's been. If she marries the prince, I will reward Runa with silver and gold and our mother's jewels. She will sit on her throne next to Prince Axel decorated as any princess should be. But if she betrays me, us, I will..."

"Jarl Roald." Thorolf approached and bowed. "Lady Runa is ready to go."

Wearing a golden-brown apron-dress underneath her fur

cloak, with her hair tightly bound in braids and covered with a blue, silk scarf, Runa looked so much like their mother. Roald nearly choked when he beheld her.

"Brother." She curtsied respectfully. "I know we haven't had much time alone. I wish to thank you for your generosity."

For a brief moment, Roald regretted his doubt in her. She looked and acted every part the true lady, a pillar of respectability and modesty, the way their father had raised her to be. She even kept her green eyes downcast while she waited for him to acknowledge her presence. But it wasn't her eyes he worried about; it was her heart.

"Rise, sweet Sister," he commanded.

She did, meeting his gaze then.

"I wish you safe travel."

"And I wish you much happiness, dear Brother."

"Do you?" He leaned in so only Runa could hear his words. "If I were to judge you at first glance, I'd have every confidence that you were a reformed woman, ready to fulfill your duty to this family. Just as you appear peaceful on the surface, so do I. But I have a war raging inside me—whether I should trust you or not."

She batted her eyelashes prettily and whispered, "Shall I rip my beating heart from my chest so you can have a spaewife read my true intentions as she would the runes?"

The stubborn girl didn't seem to understand the affect her sharp tongue had on him. The man who could seal her misfortune if she continued to defy him. Roald grinned as he drew a short knife from his weapon belt and offered it to her. "Would you like the honor of the first cut?"

"Roald? What are you doing?" Eva asked, looking from him to the weapon.

"Nothing violent, my sweetest," he lied to his wife. "I merely offered Runa a weapon for the long trip ahead. Gods forbid if she ever had to use it."

"A sage gift," Eva said.

"Yes," Runa agreed, her fake smile eating away at Roald's patience. "I thank you." She took the knife and tucked it in her own embroidered belt. "I will miss you, Sister."

Eva embraced Runa as if she'd never see the girl again. "The spirits will guide you, Runa."

Roald struggled to stay quiet as Thorolf took Runa by the elbow and guided her to the awaiting horses.

"She's a beautiful girl," Eva commented as she waved a last time to Runa. "I will miss her."

To save himself a tongue-lashing by his beloved wife, Roald waved to his sister as her mare trotted away, now knowing the girl had no intention of marrying Prince Axel.

THERE'D BE NO more begging her brother for peace. No more pleading for time. This was the first taste of freedom Runa had ever really had and she liked the way it felt. As she surveyed the beauty of the world around her, the ancient trees and rivers—the rich colors of nature—every shade of green and blue captured in Allfather's creations—it made her sad to think about how much she'd missed out on.

But the fact that she'd outmaneuvered her brother so easily made up for some of her unhappiness. Even though he'd caught her in the lie at the last minute, it was too late for him to cancel the trip.

Prince Axel would have demanded an explanation. And since Roald feared any scandals, Runa had taken advantage of her brother's weaknesses with a little help from Thorolf. She snuck a quick look in his direction, discovering that the captain was watching her.

"What troubles you?" he asked, riding closer.

"Nothing, Captain."

Thorolf sighed. "You can lie to Jarl Roald, but not to me."

"What do you mean?"

"I overheard your conversation, Lady Runa."

This news surprised her. "How? We barely breathed our words out."

"I have sharper hearing than the average man. Blame years of spying."

"This coming from the man who chided me for eavesdropping."

"'Tis not the same thing, Lady."

"No?" she teased him.

"You are too smart to think otherwise. Why did you challenge the jarl so boldly? Have you forgotten my words? That there are ways to pacify men?"

"Roald isn't a normal man, Captain Thorolf. He's a tyrant who thinks I am obligated to bend to his iron will. I cannot, will not play the spineless woman when I am so egregiously insulted. The very look on his face reveals how he truly feels about me. There is no love lost between us. Love was never a factor in our relationship."

She waited for the captain's response, eager to hear what he'd have to say. A better judge of character didn't exist, not in her small world, anyway.

"I have tried to guide you, Lady," he started, his features shadowed by disappointment. "But sometimes I think you enjoy poking the great bear with a branch of thorns just to hear him roar."

Runa pulled gently on the reins of her mare to slow the horse's gait. "And if I did, could you blame me?"

"Do you know the first rule of war?"

Runa wondered what this change in subject had to do with their current topic of conversation, but she was willing to listen. "No."

"Never give your enemy the advantage."

"Are you admitting my brother is my enemy?"

"No. But in your mind, yes."

"And what advantage have I given him exactly?"

"He knows you don't wish to marry the prince."

Runa stared at the ground, then searched the line of riders for Axel. He was positioned at the front, next to his captain. "That remains to be seen, Thorolf."

"Does it? The jarl warned me to tie you to the nearest tree whenever we made camp because he was concerned you'd run away at the first chance. Do I have reason to heed his words, Lady Runa? Will you bolt in the middle of the night like a spoiled girl or will you face your future like a woman?"

His words embarrassed her and she felt the flush creep up her neck and spread to her cheeks. "You have no cause to speak to me this way."

"I do," he insisted, grabbing the reins to her mare suddenly. "I am a simple man. My life is yours, Lady, believe me. But nothing will make me turn a blind eye if you plan on endangering yourself *and* me by breaking your word to Jarl Roald and Prince Axel. Though I serve you, I am still pledged to safeguard your welfare. To make sure you don't make foolish choices."

"Blame yourself for our current situation, Captain. You told me to visit the prince's home, to choose a suitor."

"You obviously misunderstood my heartfelt advice."

"I disagree. Look where we are. I'm no longer stuck in the great hall or in the women's quarters. I am here, free of my brother. Free of the soldiers who shadow me. Free of his scorn and suspicion."

"But not rid of me."

She'd never be free of the handsome captain. Even if she married the prince or someone else. Thorolf would haunt her for the rest of her life because she couldn't escape her unspoken feelings for him or the way her heart fluttered whenever he stared at her. But the usual fire in his eyes had been replaced by something bitter. And she couldn't stand the way it felt.

"Let go of the reins," she demanded.

"Give me a reason."

"I command you to." With that, she broke free of Thorolf's judgment and rode to the front of the line, seeking out the prince's company.

Chapter Eleven

EVERY MAN HAD LIMITS, including Thorolf. How many times had he come too close to breaking his private vow where women were concerned, especially with Runa? The godforsaken woman had his ballocks in a vice, though she didn't know it. And every time she tested his heart a little more, his raw emotions rose closer to the surface, ready to explode.

He swallowed a mouthful of warm mead from a wineskin, one of several hanging off his saddle. Good thing he'd had the sense to pack more than he usually did. Runa often inspired him to drink. Though he never got drunk. But Thorolf was blessed with a high tolerance for fermented drink. It didn't mean he couldn't appreciate the numbing effects. There was no better cure for bitterness. He took another swig, then corked the skin.

The guilt-stricken beauty had fled in shame, seeking the company of her prince. *Her prince...* A possibility that didn't please him, at all. What right did he have to feel anything one way or the other? His opinion only mattered in one capacity—as a soldier. Not as a man.

The well-traveled path they were on wound its way through the forest, the occasional clearing presenting an opportunity to make camp. They'd been on the road for several hours now, twenty people in the party, moving at a fair pace.

Thorolf circled the line many times, his trained eyes always searching the landscape for possible attackers. A soldier defended whoever he was put in charge of, he didn't fall in love with her—or lust after her—or want to kiss her pain away. His need of a wife dissolved the day his family was slaughtered and he left home, ashamed to survive the attack—broken because he couldn't save his family.

The years that had passed since then made little difference. The memory was fresh, a constant companion that nearly drove him mad every day. He could still hear his mother's agonizing screams, see her torn gown hiked up her waist, her thighs soaked with blood. His dead sire lay next to her and his eldest brother disemboweled only feet away.

Desperate to escape the moment, he dug his heels into the sides of his mount, forcing his warhorse into a frenzied gallop, leaving Prince Axel in the dust. Nothing calmed him better than the wind whipping through his hair or the sight of snow-capped peaks in the distance. For nothing reminded him more of his old home in Borg.

None in the Trondelag knew his history, but he couldn't hide his birthplace, for his accent gave it away. Thorolf's family hailed from one of the earliest settlements in Norway. Where the true dialect of his native language was still spoken, where the gods were worshipped the right way. Where women were as fierce as their men and babes were born with a sword and ax in their hands.

When his anguish and rage finally abated, he stopped abruptly. His passionate reaction to Runa and his memories reminded him why he'd worked so hard to become the kind of man he was. Strict discipline made him appear a controlled man on the outside, which allowed the chaos within to continue. Nothing would ever calm his inner turmoil. He fed off it like flames did tinder.

"Captain Thorolf?"

He twisted in the saddle to find Prince Axel riding his way. Escorting Runa did not mean he had to converse with her suitor. But to keep the peace...

"Did you see something? Someone?"

"No," Thorolf answered.

"Did you exchange unpleasant words with Lady Runa, then?"

Damn his questions. "What the lady and I discuss remains private."

"Not if it upsets her," the prince challenged.

Thorolf shifted in the saddle, the traumatized boy inside him ready to fight, ready to make Axel bleed. "There are things you don't know about her," he said with good intentions. "She's a complicated woman. Thinks too much, questions everything. Sometimes my answers don't please her."

"I am trying to know her, to unlock the secrets in her heart. But she isn't very forthcoming. I only wish to be a true confidant."

"I am glad to hear it," the captain said. "But nothing can make the lady happy until she realizes she must leave the past behind in order to claim the future."

Truer words he had never spoken, but following his own advice ... impossible.

"She still mourns the loss of her father?"

"Aye. And her mother."

"I understand." Axel inclined his head. "What of you, Captain? Why is a man of your ability escorting ladies across the country when you should be in command of a vast army?"

The prince wore no armor today, perhaps trying to impress Runa with the richly embellished tunic he donned. His stallion was equally impressive, the saddle and bridle decorated with hammered silver and amber, a testament to his wealth.

"I go where the four winds carry me."

"A man without roots."

Thorolf gritted his teeth. Those absent roots had been savagely ripped from the earth. "It is as you say."

"If you ever wish to settle in one place, Captain Thorolf, to feel a part of something greater than yourself..."

"I appreciate the thought," he said. "But I am pledged to Lady Runa. Until she releases me from her service, I will not consider any offers."

Axel squared his shoulders, his critical gaze lingering on Thorolf too long. "Don't take this as a personal insult. But if I have my way, you'll be dismissed sooner than you like." The prince turned his horse about and rode back in the direction of his guards.

Although subtle, a challenge had been made and Thorolf wouldn't forget it.

Chapter Twelve

THE NEWS OF LADY RUNA'S departure with Prince Axel worried Olvir. Not only because he wished to marry her, but his father had made it clear if he didn't, there'd be a heavy price to pay. Perhaps he'd deny him the right to his inheritance, or worse yet, deprive him of his manhood. A punishment his father had meted out on more than one occasion when a soldier or thrall had failed in their duties.

Olvir shoveled another forkful of meat into his mouth, washing it down with ale. The great hall was near empty, the men were at the practice field, except for him.

"You haven't finished your meal yet?" His father entered the room, seeking his seat at the high table.

Olvir hadn't expected to speak with his father so early. "Good day, Father," he said with stiff courtesy. "I was just about to go." He stood.

"Wait." Jarl Otkel eyed his trencher. "You'd waste my food, boy? There's half a chicken on that platter."

"I only wished..."

"To run and hide?"

"To spare you further disappointment."

Otkel picked up a loaf of bread and tore it in half, shoving a piece in his mouth. "If that was a regular concern of yours, my son, you wouldn't be here, you'd be outside learning to swing a sword or aim an ax."

"If the necessity arises, Father, I will pick up a weapon and defend our home. Until then, I prefer the peace of my manuscripts or managing your gold." Always obedient to his sire's wishes, Olvir knew what he risked by refusing to be a soldier. "I could be quite useful to you if you'd trust me, Sir."

"No," Otkel snapped. "Leave the management of my holdings to the old men who are too weak to serve as soldiers. You may read and write in the secrecy of your chamber, away from probing eyes. But in the open, you will pretend to be a man as best you can." He stared at his son. "Stand up."

He turned away sharply, wishing to be back in Northumbria where Prince Ivarr had a legitimate use for his skills.

"Did you hear me, Boy?"

"Yes, Father."

"Then do it."

Olvir shoved his chair away from the table with his feet, then rose.

"Where is your weapon belt?"

"I don't own one anymore."

"Your sword?"

"In my chamber."

The jarl's gaze swept over him disapprovingly. "Tell me you keep a knife strapped to your calf."

"All right, Sir. I keep a knife strapped to my calf."

"Damn you, Boy. Do you think I'm incapable of detecting the sarcasm in your voice?"

He shook his head. "Hardly, Sir. Nothing escapes you."

"That's right." His father tasted the roasted bird on his platter and smiled. "One of the only things that still pleases me, good food."

Olvir sat back down, quite annoyed. Instead of wasting his

talents here, he wished to be anywhere else and even had considered selling his skills to another jarl. "I have failed you once again."

"Yes," his sire agreed. "But there is still something you can do to make up for all of it."

Olvir knew what is was. Produce an heir who could be raised a warrior. "If I am to take a wife, I must find a suitable woman to marry."

Jarl Otkel used a thin splinter of wood to pick the food from his teeth. "Search no further than Jarl Roald's longhouse. Runa is my choice for you, for this family."

"I am sorry…" He hesitated to break the bad news to him, but didn't see a way out of the conversation. "The lady has departed for the northlands with Prince Axel, one of the suitors her brother has deemed an appropriate husband."

The dead silence that followed scared Olvir more than his father's booming voice.

Two meaty fists finally hit the tabletop. "What are you saying?"

"Lady Runa is no longer in the Trondelag."

"Goddamn it," Otkel swore. "If you'd done what I told you the night you were in Roald's hall, there'd be no question who the lady should marry."

"I don't rape women."

"No," his sire said. "You *are* one."

Olvir laughed then, without restraint. A full-bellied chuckle that felt better than anything he'd done in quite a while.

Otkel's eyes narrowed. "The sound of a madman if I've ever heard one."

"No, Father. The sound of a man who has nothing left to lose. I am a burden. A disgrace. A female dressed in men's garb. A plague and curse. The very end of your bloodline. So why not hang me now and get the inevitable over with? Kill me and marry a young, fertile bride who will give you many sons. With me out of the way, your new son would be your heir."

His father's confused expression only made him laugh harder.

"Be careful what you wish for, Boy."

"Why?" Olvir challenged. "I've made my wish clear. Death brings peace, Father. Freedom from this living Hel I've endured since I was old enough to walk and talk around you. Desperate men have no expectations. And if I thought there'd be a chance of me being admitted to God's glorious kingdom by taking my own life, I'd gladly slit my wrists and bleed out here and now."

"You'd die a coward's death to escape me?"

"I'd just die, Father. Willingly. Gratefully."

"Shit on your life then." The jarl shot up from his seat. "Here." He ripped a blade from the sheath on his hip and tossed it on the table in front of Olvir. "It takes real courage to die, Boy, no matter the method. So prove me wrong for once. Show me what kind of man you truly are. Earn my respect back. And once you breathe your last, I'll bury you like a king."

Olvir's breath came hard and heavy as he contemplated his next move. The smooth steel tempted him greatly. It would be a quick end, plunging the point into his heart.

"Well?" his sire said.

Determined, Olvir grabbed the knife off the table. He inspected the blade, even tested the end with his finger. It drew blood and Olvir wiped his hand on his braies. He stood, then walked around the table, stepping off the dais. He faced his sire and dropped to his knees.

"Is this what you want to see, Father? Now you'll have a reason to mock me when you sit around the hearth at night with your captains. You can tell them I went happily, though, ready to meet the One True God. Not Odin or Thor."

Olvir raised his hand, still unsure where to aim the blade. If he chose his heart, he'd die quickly. But if he pierced his gut, he'd bleed slowly, having time to enjoy the look of shock on his father's face when he realized he'd actually done it.

"Forgive me, Mother," Olvir whispered as he brought the knife down.

"Sniveling fool…" His sire dove over the table and landed on top of Olvir, knocking the blade from his unsteady hand.

Olvir struggled to breathe as his father straddled his chest.

"You want to die?" Olvir turned his head, not wanting to face his sire. "Don't you know by revealing this secret you've given me every reason to make you live?" This time his father was the one to laugh.

Helpless under his father's heavy weight, Olvir closed his eyes and prayed for relief. To any God who would listen.

Chapter Thirteen

RUNA BALANCED THE TRENCHER on her knees as she tasted the bread and cheese her maid had served her. Prince Axel sat with his captains on the other side of the campfire, his gaze rarely leaving her. By choice, Runa shared a corner with Captain Thorolf and the other guards he'd chosen.

"You see the way he stares at you?" Thorolf said between bites of food. "That's a man marked by love—I know the look well."

Runa wasn't used to hearing the captain speak so freely in front of others. But she welcomed the conversation tonight, feeling unusually lonely. "Do you speak from experience?"

"Not my own," he assured her. "My men's… Which is why I must encourage you to put an end to all this nonsense."

"Nonsense?"

"Yes, Lady Runa. As we've discussed before, we're now three days into the journey and the man is becoming more territorial and obsessed with you. By the time we reach his home, he'll never allow you out of his sight. What am I to do when it's time to return to the Trondelag? Twould be better for you not to speak to the man the rest of the way."

"Am I to blame?" She knew the answer, but wanted to hear Thorolf admit that her brother forced her hand in this venture. "Should I be disagreeable then? Give Axel every reason not to like my company?"

Thorolf sighed and set his empty platter on the ground. "This conversation seems to go in circles, Lady. I find I have to keep repeating myself in order to make you understand anything I'm trying to explain. I recognize the unfairness of Jarl Roald's demands in your eyes. There's naught to be done about it. The laws and traditions of our people allow for jarls to forge alliances through marriages. You aren't the first, nor the last sister who will shoulder this responsibility."

Runa shrugged. In that moment, she cared little for what other women had done. All that mattered was the unhappiness she faced. Didn't a woman of reasonable intelligence have the right to question the choices made on her behalf? To express her own desires for the future? To serve the gods? "I appreciate your effort, Captain Thorolf. And since you know my deepest secrets, I am able to be completely honest with you. Something I treasure greatly, believe me."

She looked up at him as he stretched his arms above his head, his muscular torso and arms something to be deeply admired.

"Roald refuses to release me from the fate-binding with my brother, Konal. Think what it would feel like to face that sort of responsibility. The kind of pressure I am under. The very idea that anything I say or do could possibly alter Konal's happy life. Is this how a jarl usually demonstrates his wisdom and power? Tell me."

Sighing, Thorolf reached for his wineskin. "I admit fate-binding is a timeworn practice, something I have never personally seen until now."

"That's good to hear, Captain. For if fate-binding is archaic, so must arranged marriages be."

He swallowed a surprising amount of mead before he lowered the skin from his lips. He sat back down on a felled tree, visibly annoyed. "Is this how you've acted all your life, Lady? Arguing about anything you disagree with?"

"When it involves my own life, yes."

"Tis no wonder Jarl Roald wishes to see you settled elsewhere."

Runa's mouth dropped open, shocked at his brutal honesty. This was the first time he'd ever been critical of her. "I offered my brother a respectable alternative. The temple is a fair distance from the Trondelag. And if we look at it from a different perspective, a marriage of sorts."

Thorolf smirked. "Will you consummate this supposed marriage with a stone effigy? Take your choice, there are dozens at the temple."

He'd been to the temple? When? "It seems too much mead has made you forget who you address, Captain."

"I disagree. If anything, it provides clarity. Did we not make the same arrangement I had with your brother? To always speak frankly?"

"Aye," she admitted, eager to question him about the holy place she'd dreamt of visiting since childhood. "I've grown up under the sharp eye of a father who disliked me and, now, a brother who'd sooner sell me to a rich husband than consider my feelings. Whenever someone is unfairly skeptical of me, I inadvertently jump to my own defense. There are very few people I consider true friends. You see, Captain, most people are more concerned with pleasing the jarl, to see what favors or rewards they can get. I know you are not one of them."

"I am your friend, Runa. Odin give me strength for it. Or strike me dead. I care..." He stopped talking suddenly.

"What?" Runa asked, not recognizing the emotion on his face—as if an unsavory thought had popped into his head and he didn't want to finish what he was thinking or feeling. "Do you regret caring, Captain? Is that it?"

Too many times of late she'd seen the fire in his eyes extinguished by something that seemed to trouble him. "You're free to resort back to that stoic soldier I know you to be. Treat me as you would any other noble, Thorolf. Serve as expected, and when the day is over and your duties complete, gather round the fire with your brethren and complain about me. It won't hurt me much. I've overheard plenty of the men in service to my family curse us after too much mead or ale has loosened their ungrateful tongues."

Thorolf rubbed his temples and looked her directly in the eyes. "Do you think I'd ever insult you?"

She considered it. "No."

"Then why give life to such vile thoughts?"

"I-I..." Because she needed to hear him say how much he cared ... fantasied that he loved her ... wanted him to drop on one knee and pledge aloud so the whole world could hear, that he'd serve her faithfully forever. "I have little confidence in my own worth, Sir. It is difficult to believe a man of your caliber truly cares for me or even considers what I have to say of any value."

Thorolf nodded as if he understood. "With me, have no doubt."

"I will try to remember."

The captain angled his head toward the prince. "I am sure Prince Axel feels the same."

"How lucky am I?" she asked, following his gaze to the prince. "There are two flesh and blood men who care about me."

At that moment, something stirred Axel's men keeping watch over the encampment. A call went out to ready weapons and Thorolf jumped into action, corralling Runa and her maid behind him.

He pointed at one of his men. "Go and find out what's wrong."

"Are we in danger?" Runa asked.

"Something is out there or someone." He scanned the perimeter. "We will take no chances, though. Move to the trees." He pointed. "Hallam, Aril. Take up position on either side, I will man the front."

Within seconds, Runa found herself surrounded by men with their swords and shields at the ready for a fight.

After what seemed a long time, Prince Axel and three of his guards joined them. "Fear not, Lady Runa. We have unexpected company."

Thorolf stood down then, but didn't sheathe his weapon.

"Who?" she asked, stepping away from the protective cover of the trees.

"Someone I'm sure you don't want to see again."

"My brother?" she blurted without thinking.

Axel gave her an appraising look, then smiled. "Sibling rivalry seems to plague every family, no matter how small or large."

"Yes," she said, rewarding him with a wide grin, welcoming his understanding. "If not Roald, who?"

"Yes," Thorolf interjected. "Who would join us on the road?"

"Jarl Skrymir," Axel said.

"May the bastard never share another woman's bed..." Thorolf raked his fingers through his hair, his handsome features twisted with rage and hatred. "Where is he?"

Axel squeezed Thorolf's shoulder. "I, too, question his motive for showing up uninvited."

"I am glad," the captain said. "But my fight with him was

never finished the night he insulted Lady Runa at the feast. I will handle this." He stormed off before she could say a word.

"The captain cares for you," Axel observed.

"Aye," she said, still looking in the direction Thorolf had gone. "He is like a brother to me."

"A brother?" The prince sounded skeptical.

Runa faced him then. "Have we given you cause to think otherwise?"

"No." Axel shifted on his feet. "My eyes see one thing, Lady. My conscience another."

Chapter Fourteen

THOROLF APPROACHED WHERE JARL SKRYMIR stood with a stag draped across his shoulders. The prince's men hadn't granted him access to the camp yet. If the captain had his way, Skrymir would be turned away.

Four stakes had been hammered into the ground at the opening of the clearing, burning torches hung at the top. The sentries held their positions there and Skrymir looked too comfortable waiting to be invited to the fire.

"Captain Thorolf," the bastard greeted. "How fortunate we've crossed paths again."

Thorolf snorted. "Depends on who you ask."

The jarl looked left, then right. "You are the only man standing before me."

"Aye. If I had a choice, I'd be the last."

Skrymir tsked. "My presence displeases you?"

"Your presence revolts me, as did your words to Lady Runa."

With ease, Skrymir lifted the stag off his shoulders and tossed it on the ground. "A gift for the lady. Fresh venison is always preferable over dried fish and bread."

Thorolf eyed the offering with distaste. He'd die before he let Runa eat anything provided by this miscreant. Rage overtook him and Thorolf walked over to the carcass and spat on it, then stepped on the hindquarter, grounding it into the dirt with the heel of his boot. He met Skrymir's gaze, silently daring him to make a move. "The lady has eaten her fill already."

There were half a dozen armed men with Skrymir. Easily outnumbered by the eighteen in Prince Axel's party. But Thorolf wasn't interested in a full battle. He wanted to face this man one-on-one.

"What would your master say about such behavior?" Skrymir taunted.

"I am a freeman," Thorolf informed him. "Responsible for my own choices."

"A commoner, nonetheless."

"A man."

Skrymir laughed and his men with him.

The cold steel at Thorolf's hip was hard to resist. He flexed his fingers, instinct challenging him to draw his weapon. *Humiliate him. Destroy him. Spill his blood.* "Why are you here?"

"To see Lady Runa."

"She has made her choice ... there is nothing left to say. Take your paltry gift and go."

Skrymir glared at him and reached for his sword. Thorolf moved quickly, unsheathing his weapon first and laying the blade across the jarl's chest before he could challenge Thorolf.

"Give me a reason to cut you," the captain growled. "Utter another word and I will, regardless of the penalty."

"Captain Thorolf!"

He didn't need to turn around to know who called his name—Prince Axel.

"What is this about?" the prince asked.

Thorolf didn't move. "Ask your guest."

"Jarl Skrymir? Why did you come here?" Axel inquired.

"I will hunt you down and kill you one day," Skrymir whispered so only Thorolf could hear him. "Look for me on a night you least expect it, when your belly is full, your pikk happily sheathed in the woman you love. Then I will strike…"

"I await your answer…" the prince pressed.

Skrymir raised his chin. "There is only one road leading north, Prince Axel. When I realized who we came upon, I decided to share my kill." He motioned at the stag on the ground. "Fresh meat is surely welcome in this camp."

"Aye. As long as your intentions are peaceful, you may eat with us. Captain Thorolf, lower your weapon, let this man pass."

Outranked, Thorolf obeyed his host. Regardless of his personal hatred for Skrymir, the man had done nothing wrong here, *yet*. As the guest of a prince, he must respect Axel's commands, unless Runa was in danger. Then he'd wage war on anyone who got in the way.

As he turned, he caught Runa staring at him, unable to interpret her expression. What did she think about his confrontation with Skrymir? How much had she witnessed? Did it matter? She knew he'd protect her. Relief flooded through him when she nodded. Not the reaction he'd hoped for, but since she was with two men of power, both interested in signing a marriage contract with her and forging an alliance with her brother, protocol must be adhered to. His personal opinion mattered little in the lady's affairs now. But damn it, the more time he spent with her, the more he disliked the whole idea of her choosing a husband.

"YOU MUST ACT quickly," Runa's maid, Auda, warned as she joined Thorolf near the fire.

Thorolf regarded the older woman. "Why do you speak to

me now? We've been on the road for days and you've never made an effort to even say good morn."

"There was nothing worthwhile to say." She gestured across the way where her mistress sat between Axel and Skrymir, looking as if she was enjoying all the attention. "One of those wolves will sink his teeth into her soon enough."

The captain didn't need to be reminded and waved the maid off. "Go back to your tent." He took a swig of mead. "Lady Runa is more capable of fending for herself than any other woman I've met. My protest would fall on deaf ears."

Auda harrumphed. "She is headstrong and much younger than you, Captain Thorolf. And this..." She moved with remarkable speed and snatched the wineskin from his hand. "Will only muddle your head."

He growled at her, not needing to be mothered. "Have I ever failed at my duties?"

"Never. But why start now?"

He didn't understand. "The prince and jarl are within easy striking distance. My men are strategically positioned. What more can I give her?"

Auda sat down next to him. "Your heart."

"Mistress Auda," he said out of respect for her age. "I have no heart to give."

She put a hand on his shoulder, slapping something against his chest with the other. Whatever it was fell on his lap and he looked down, a leather bag.

"If you hadn't a heart, Captain, you'd be incapable of loving her the way you do."

"Love her? Lady Runa?" Heat surged through his body. "And what do you know of love?"

"Three sons and a daughter say I know plenty."

He admired her spirit and laughed. "Aye, it seems I misjudged you."

"I forgive you, Captain. Now open the bag and throw the runes."

No. He never consulted the runes or got involved with witches. Nothing good could come out of knowing the future. Men were meant to live in the moment, fate bringing what it did. Only the gods knew the future.

He tossed the bag to her. "I've no use for magic."

"Magic? Do I look like a spaewife?"

"Ask me not, old woman. I've already made a fool of myself by not realizing you had a family."

"Gaze upon me again, Thorolf."

He looked up and nearly jumped out of his skin. The same woman he'd spoken with a breath ago didn't occupy the spot next to him now. Instead, a young redhead with a beautiful face smiled at him.

"Magic is what you believe it to be, Captain. Now blink your eyes thrice."

He followed her instructions. When he risked a second look in her direction, Auda had returned to her regular form. He rubbed his eyes vigorously, just to make sure he wasn't hallucinating. "What tricks do you play, woman?"

"Toss the runes, Captain."

He scooped the bag up, opened it, poured the runes into his palm, then gave them a good shake before he dropped them on the ground. Nine distinct symbols waited for interpretation.

"Nine stones to represent the nine realms," Auda explained. She scooted off the rocks and squatted in front of the runes, inspecting them closely. "You are a man of mystery, Captain." She gazed at him. "There's an unnatural fire burning in your belly—one that requires feeding in the way of blood. Weregild will never satisfy your need for revenge, will it?"

How did she know? "What are you about?" he asked, suspicious of her intent.

"Truth, Thorolf. Simple truth."

The warmth of Runa's laughter wrapped around him then, spiking the jealousy inside him. He closed his eyes, searching for control, hoping he could hold his temper back.

"Beware of things to come," she continued. "Trickery and violence. Death for many."

Unable to tolerate more of her riddles, he gripped her shoulders and spun her around. "Speak plainly, woman."

"You love Lady Runa. Protect her from these men. Take her away before it's too late. The dark one is evil."

If he weren't an honorable man, he'd squeeze the rest of the truth out of her. "Leave me."

"But I wasn't finished."

"I am," he said in a low tone. "Go."

"As you wish, Captain." She gathered the runes and put them back in the leather bag. "Odin be with you."

Chapter Fifteen

Outwardly, Runa must appear happy to entertain Prince Axel and Jarl Skrymir. However, the dark lord made her feel anxious and uncomfortable. Twice his arm brushed against hers, whether intentional or not. Her first loyalty was with Axel, if only for the sake of duty. She wanted nothing to do with Skrymir. His intent was clear. If she married him, she'd serve one purpose, a mere vessel to carry his unborn children.

"Tell me why you left the comfort and safety of the Trondelag to brave the wilds, Lady Runa," the jarl asked between sips of mead.

The man tried too hard to make casual conversation.

"I asked to see Prince Axel's homeland. The way he described it piqued my deepest interest. Sometimes words don't do a place justice."

"Aye," Skrymir agreed. "I've been along the borders of the prince's holdings. Few places rival it for beauty, I admit. But my lands provide natural barriers that few enemies would brave."

"Perhaps the better choice is to make peace with your rivals so you don't have to worry so much over who would try to take what is yours," Runa suggested.

"A woman's foolish dream," Skrymir said. "Even in the crags among the highest peaks lurk unknown dangers. Tribesmen from the oldest people who occupied this country long before our gods ever breathed life into the Norse."

"Or a Swedish prince," Axel added as he drank from a silver cup. "I prefer peace over war, Lady Runa. It costs much less to make treaties than it does to bury the dead."

"You grow weary of battle?" the jarl questioned Axel.

"No," he said dryly. "I wield my ax when I must. Shed blood when it is necessary to defend my home. When you are a foreigner, it takes careful diplomacy to convince the native people how truly dedicated you are to their best interests and safety. If I hadn't inherited my father's good political instincts, I fear I wouldn't be able to offer this lovely woman a new place to call home." The prince gave Runa a warm smile, his eyes filled with adoration.

"Has the lady accepted your troth?"

Axel looked to Runa for an answer.

"Nay," Runa said gently. "But I am considering it, wholeheartedly." She didn't want to embarrass the prince in front of his rival.

Just then, Skrymir's servants arrived with platters of fresh meat and wineskins. The jarl rubbed his hands together. "A feast fit for a lady."

Runa accepted a trencher and smelled the roasted venison with pleasure. Fresh onions and herbs had been added to a dark gravy. "Thank you for your generosity, Jarl Skrymir."

He grinned. "Tis a pleasure to break bread with you again."

Hungrier than she had thought, Runa ate with purpose, not wasting a mouthful. She dipped bread in the gravy and savored the rich broth. Though Jarl Skrymir made her squirm, he surely kept a capable cook, even on the road.

Minutes after the prince and his guards had finished eating, washing the meat down with wine, the first moans of pain sounded from beyond the fire. Runa ignored it at first, thinking some of the guards were fighting or had overindulged in drink. But when a bloodcurdling scream came, the hair on the back of her neck stood on end and she jumped up from her seat.

"What is wrong?" she questioned worriedly, eyeing first the prince, then Skrymir. "Should we not investigate?"

"Be at ease," Skrymir said matter-of-fact. "Soon it will be all over."

"W-what are you talking about?"

Prince Axel suddenly gripped his throat with both hands, staggering to his feet, the empty trencher falling from his lap. "What have you done?" he asked Skrymir. "What treachery have you brought into my camp?" He wavered, nearly falling, but managed to pull his sword. "Come and stand behind me, Runa. Now."

She did as he commanded, fear sending a frigid chill up her spine. *Dear Odin, spare the prince. Please.*

Much to her surprise, Skrymir kept his place, licking the juice from his fingers as if nothing had happened. "There is nothing you can do, Prince Axel. No help for you or your guards. In fact, I suggest you sit back down. The more excitable you become, the quicker the poison will kill you."

"Poison?" Runa shrieked. "W-why? What wrong have I or the prince done you? Were you not welcomed into my brother's home? Offered every comfort?" Her own throat started to tighten.

"I did not poison you, dear Runa. Only my rival. You better wish him well in the afterlife. A man poisoned will never see the gates of Valhalla. He will roam the endless underworld, Hel his assured destination."

Desperation consumed her as she begged the prince to turn around. "Please. Let me help you." She gripped his shoulders from behind. "I am sorry … so very sorry this evil man has followed me here. Forgive me..."

Axel faced her then and cupped her cheek with his big hand. "Tis no fault of yours. I welcomed this man into my camp. And I'd do it again if it meant I could spend another day in your company."

Tears stung Runa's eyes.

"You are treasured, Runa." The prince placed his hand over his heart. "Now do me one last honor..."

"Anything," she whispered.

He leaned close. "Run."

She hesitated, her gaze flicking to Skrymir, who still sat in place, unconcerned, an arrogant bastard—a ruthless murderer.

"Now..." the prince commanded, wheeling about with his sword held high.

This time she responded quickly, disappearing through an opening between the trees, hoping she'd survive long enough to make it home and beg her brother to avenge the prince's death.

CONSUMED BY JEALOUSY, Thorolf had retired to his tent once he was convinced Runa was safe. But when screams sounded, he awoke in a stupor and stumbled out of his shelter, his ax in hand. Chaos had erupted everywhere, his own men missing. He called for them, hoping they were nearby. No answer came.

He edged forward, entering the clearing, shocked to see a dozen of Prince Axel's men crawling and gripping their sides in obvious pain, several throwing up. Had the water or food been tainted? Perhaps the mead or wine had gone bad? He rushed to the closest guard and turned him over, only to find blood seeping out of his nostrils and lips. *Fuck.*

Frustrated and worried, Thorolf went to the next man, only to find him in the same condition. He gave the man a firm shake, hoping to bring him out of his daze. "What happened? Where is the prince? Lady Runa?"

The warrior struggled to draw a breath, but his eyes were clearly focused on Thorolf. "Meat," he whispered. "The food..."

The captain didn't need to hear more and gently lowered the man to the ground and whispered a blessing over him. There was nothing he could do to save the guard. But nothing could stop him from avenging the warrior's violent end. Rage gripped Thorolf as he stalked forward, one name on his lips. "Skrymir," he roared, searching the area for Runa. If one hair on her head had been moved out of place, one threatening word uttered in her direction, he'd slice through the bastard jarl slowly, making sure he suffered for agonizing hours.

"Skrymir!" he yelled again.

This time the dark lord came into view. "Captain Thorolf, I'm glad you are awake and able to join the festivities."

"Where is Runa?" he demanded, gripping his ax handle, itching to strike.

"Gone. Disappeared into the night while I watched Prince Axel die."

"What have you done here?" Thorolf asked, needing an explanation for this senseless slaughter as he drew closer to his target. "Why have you killed these men?"

"To eliminate my competition," the jarl said plainly. "I will wed Runa, no matter what I have to do to claim her."

"This is cowardice, the kind of underhanded attack you'd expect from a woman, not a jarl. Not a man who keeps the ways of the gods."

"Didn't I tell you, Captain Thorolf? I care little for what Allfather demands. I live for myself."

Thorolf growled, only feet from his enemy. "Face me."

Skrymir chuckled. "I already am."

Something blunt hit the back of Thorolf's head, skull-splitting pain followed and he sunk to his knees, seeing white spots before his eyes. He groaned, struggling to stay awake.

"Your end is near." Skrymir stood over him now. "Don't fight the urge to pass out or more pain will follow." He kicked Thorolf in the ribs. "Twould have been better if you'd eaten the meat. Now I'm afraid you must suffer..."

Another blow to the head came and the captain finally surrendered to the darkness.

Chapter Sixteen

RUNA RAN AS fast as she could. Terrified for Thorolf and the prince, she didn't know what to do or where to go. Just deeper into the darkness—away from Jarl Skrymir—away from the danger. Why hadn't she paid closer attention to Skrymir? The way he conveniently showed up, how he made the offering of the stag, it all made sense now. He'd likely planned this from the moment she left the Trondelag.

Out of breath, she finally stopped. A half-moon shined overhead, silvery light breaking through the thick canopy. The forest held everything she needed for survival. Konal had taught her that from a young age. She could make it for days if all she had to think about was herself. But more than a dozen men were counting on her to bring help. Not that she thought they had a chance really. Skrymir didn't seem the kind of man to leave any witnesses behind.

And soon enough, he'd come after her.

Regret deepened her sorrow as she sank to her knees out of exhaustion. Why would the gods curse such loyal followers? Only she deserved to be punished for toying with the prince's heart and lying to her brother. For taking Thorolf's advice and twisting it to suit her selfish needs.

"Please, great Odin..." she begged aloud. "Give me the will to find help, to make my way out of these woods." Once she finished her prayer, she stood, listening closely for any unusual noises. But only silence greeted her.

The mountains were to the north, that much she remembered, and the temple ... eastward. She'd studied the maps in Roald's solar whenever she had a chance to sneak inside. For years she'd been memorizing the layout of the lands around her home. If she closed her eyes now, she could picture everything clearly. She might be able to find her way to the temple. It was worth a chance.

In the gloom, Runa did just that—picked her way through the forest. Hours passed as she walked, hoping to meet someone. She cared little for her own safety, it was only the hope that Thorolf and some of the other men had survived that kept her moving. The captain had been strangely absent from the campfire tonight. Maybe his confrontation with Jarl Skrymir made him want to be alone. Or the fact that Runa had played her part so convincingly with Axel, that he could no longer stand the sight of her.

"Thorolf..." she whispered, hope and foreboding mingling together inside her heart. "I want to see you again—need to."

As soon as she uttered the words, she emerged from the forest and spotted a fire somewhere ahead. Many fires ... perhaps a big camp or the temple? Odin willing... With renewed faith, she ran blindly, letting the flicker of light guide her feet. Everything happened for a reason.

Something invisible pulled her closer and closer to the light.

Dozens of torch stands surrounded the base of a rocky incline and groups of men hovered around open fires. By the light of those torches, she could see a footpath climbing the hill. At the top, the outline of a wood and stone structure. Odin be praised! She'd reached the temple. Tears streamed down her face as she knelt, feeling a sense of completion. All her life she'd dreamt of this moment, wondered what it would feel like to behold the holiest of places in her country. Norsemen of every background gathered here every nine years to honor the gods through oath making and blood sacrifices—sometimes human.

She struggled feebly with the explosion of emotions inside. Should she take the time to make a sacrifice or rush to the temple and seek help? No one had ever told her the proper protocol for such an occasion. Where innocent life was at stake, she was willing to risk trusting her own instincts.

As she approached the trailhead, one of the guards looked at her. "Where did you come from, Girl?"

Should she lie to protect herself? No, only the truth would do now. She'd deceived so many people for so long she was starting to believe her own lies. "My name is Lady Runa, sister of Jarl Roald from the Trondelag. I am in dire need of help. I narrowly escaped an attack by Jarl Skrymir in the forest. He followed Prince Axel and my personal guard across the northlands, bent on murder. I'm afraid he has killed many. There was nowhere else for me to go."

The guard immediately stood, his interest increased tenfold. "Prince Axel?"

"Aye." She trembled all over then. "I fear he's dead, Sir."

The guard regarded her for a long moment. "Come with me."

Runa followed him up the steep pathway, lit torches attached to a wood handrail provided ample light. By the time they reached the top of the hill, she was out of breath.

"Purify yourself before entering Odin's temple," the guard commanded.

The wooden eaves which seemed to run the length of the longhouse were ornately carved, the faces of the gods she held so dear stared back at her. Dragonheads and other mythical creatures were also honored in the carvings, the oak double doors inscribed with runic symbols. Some she could decipher; others were as foreign to her as Latin.

"How?" The very idea of standing in the doorway to the temple raised gooseflesh all over her tired body.

He gaped at her in surprise. "By whispering words of praise—or seeking forgiveness if that's what it takes."

Closing her eyes tight, she mumbled a half-hearted prayer. She'd make it up to the gods another time. Speaking to someone to rally enough guards to go rescue Thorolf and whatever men were left alive was more pressing. After what seemed an acceptable amount of time, she opened her eyes.

"I am done."

The sentry nodded, then opened the doors leading inside the great structure.

She walked across the threshold of the circular room in awe. Thick, dark wood beams crisscrossed overhead. Nine hearths warmed the room, each tended by a maiden wearing silk robes with their long hair cascading over their shoulders. These were the temple maidens, the faceless sisters she'd fantasized about joining. At the center of the chamber stood a dais shaded by an ancient oak tree whose branches reached the rafters above.

Tapestries depicting runic symbols decorated the curved walls and covered the stone floor. Did she deserve to be here? Would Allfather strike her dead for daring to enter his sanctuary with a black heart? Men had died because of her untruths. Quite possibly, the man she secretly loved. And the honorable Prince Axel.

"Keep moving, Girl," the guard urged. "The priest will welcome you."

She gazed at the guard, licking her dry lips. "W-where do I go?"

"Approach the altar." He pointed toward the dais. "Hidden by Thor's holy oak."

Slowly and reverent of where she walked, Runa made her way to the tree.

"Closer, Girl," a voice directed her.

A tall, bald man wearing a purple tunic and carrying a carved staff appeared from beneath the lowest branches. The left side of his face was tattooed with runic symbols, like the ones on the tapestries.

"I saw your tears in a dream, tasted your despair," he said. "The day of reckoning has come for you, Lady Runa. You must choose your fate wisely—will you serve the gods or love a man?"

Stunned by the priest's revelation, she froze, unable to form words in her mind.

"There's nothing to fear here," he informed her. "Odin speaks to men in different ways. You are no different than many of the girls who seek shelter here."

"B-but…"

"Guilt is the first step toward healing," he said. "I will sacrifice a dove on your behalf. Blood will satisfy Allfather, for now."

Runa hit her knees in supplication. What else could she do in the presence of such a holy man? In the shadow of the great altar? "In the name of Jarl Roald, son of Brandr, lord in the Trondelag, I beg for sanctuary and assistance with bringing Jarl Skrymir to justice for his deception and murder of innocent men."

The priest leaned on his staff and stepped forward. "Murder?"

"He poisoned Prince Axel and his men and Captain Thorolf and my personal guards."

"Did you see him do it?"

"Aye," she said. "He confessed to Prince Axel as he was dying."

"What motive did Jarl Skrymir have?'

Runa stared at the floor, ashamed to look him in the eyes. "Me," she choked out.

"You?"

"Aye."

"And why would a man as powerful as Jarl Skrymir seek out a lowlander like you?"

This time before she spoke, she raised her chin. "To forge an alliance with my brother through marriage."

"Why kill your men if he wanted to marry you?"

"I rejected the jarl's suit. I was journeying with Prince Axel to his home for an extended visit."

"To marry him?"

"No," she said.

The priest's eyebrows jutted up in confusion.

"I didn't wish to marry anyone."

"I see," he said gently. "Odin speaks to your heart?"

"Every night."

"Will you take vows?"

"No," she said. "Please—let us not wait any longer." Heart pounding, Runa managed to bow even lower to the floor. "I beg for your mercy."

"Gjest," the priest said. "If this girl speaks truth, a great wrong has been committed. Gather fifteen guards and the necessary horses and ride with her to the place where this supposed crime happened. If you find no evidence supporting her claim, execute her immediately. But if she speaks honestly, do what you must to aid her people."

She stood then. "Thank you."

"Do not be so quick to thank me. Payment will be collected,

either in blood or gold." He closed the distance between them and reached for her forehead, tracing a shape on her skin. "Allfather preserve you on your journey back."

Chapter Seventeen

THE SCENT OF wet earth welcomed Thorolf when he opened his eyes. Face down in the mud, he groaned as he rolled onto his back, heavy rain hitting his face. Pain radiated from his head to his legs. The last thing he remembered was Skrymir standing over him and then kicking him in the ribs. The world had gone dark after that. As he touched the back of his head and felt an egg-sized knot, he knew why.

"Son of a whore…" he cursed, eyeing the blood on his fingers. He'd likely need stiches.

A rolling thunder of hatred inside gave him the strength he needed to sit up. Judging by the position of the sun, it was still early morning. Skrymir was long gone. Filthy coward. With some difficulty, Thorolf staggered to his feet, feeling off-balance but capable of taking a few steps. Bodies were strewn everywhere. But Thorolf was only interested in finding one person—Runa.

He searched the camp, even her tent. Not a trace of the lady or her maid. But he did find the three guards he'd handpicked, all dead. Axel's men were all accounted for, too. However, the prince's body was missing. Had Runa and Axel fled together? Possibly made it to safety under the cover of night? Thorolf prayed for it to be so.

Whether he wanted to or not, he must do the right thing by

these men. Leaving them to rot would be wrong. He raked his fingers through his wet hair, lifted his chin, and let the heavy rain cleanse his face. There was only one way to make up for his mistake last night. Only one way to earn his honor back after allowing jealousy to cloud his judgment. Kill Skrymir.

Nothing would keep him from it.

Whatever had come over him while he watched Runa entertaining her two suitors last night had made him sick. He sought comfort in a wineskin, drinking three times the amount he ever had, hoping to wash away any trace of love he had for the girl. It didn't work. The drunker he got, the more intense his feelings became. All he could see and hear was Runa. That mischievous smile. Her green eyes. That perfect body.

Roald's words came to mind. *Odin save the man who ever truly loves her.* Little did his jarl know, that blessing was meant for him. For Thorolf loved her—deeply. Obsessively so. Enough to kill for her. Enough to die to avenge her.

But first…

Ignoring the pain in his head, he started to gather the bodies. Too wet to start a funeral fire, he'd cover the corpses with tent material to keep the rain off. He'd come back later to honor each man in the right way. Maybe with help. And if not, he'd meet them in Valhalla or Hel.

It took over an hour to complete his first task. Then he stripped his ruined clothes off and bathed in the nearby creek, eyeing the bruises on his torso as he scrubbed the dry blood away. Nothing seemed broken. But bruised ribs were more painful than most sword wounds. Once he finished, he went to his tent and dressed in a fresh tunic and braies, then put his weapon belt on. The horses were scattered, but his mount was well trained and knew to come when whistled for.

Ready to go, he eyed the encampment a last time, guilt

weighing heavy in his gut. If he'd thought with his head instead of his heart this would have never happened. Runa would be safe and with him still.

A chill crept down his spine then. Where should he check first? There was a village a few miles from here. Or should he ride to the temple? Hundreds of armed men provided security for the priests. Surely they'd help him. And if Runa was alive, she'd seek sanctuary there. He climbed into the saddle and nudged his horse eastward, to the complex where the gods were rumored to live.

THOROLF MET WITH some resistance at the double doors that opened into the temple. Four guards armed with pikes, crossed their weapons to bar his way inside.

"Let me pass," he commanded, the expressionless, possibly mindless men only stared ahead. "I am Captain Thorolf from the Trondelag. I have business with the priests."

The doors opened finally and a man greeted him from behind the weapons. "Good morn, sir," he said. "We are unable to admit anyone into the sanctuary without good cause."

Thorolf didn't blame the scribe for following orders, but by law, the place should be accessible to everyone at all times of the day and night. "What reason do you have to keep me outside?"

"A breach in security."

"Someone threatened the priests?"

In the old days, when Thorolf still lived among his people in Borg, it was considered an honor to be chosen for the temple guard. A responsibility shared by the northern chieftains. Any threat to the holy men felt very personal to Thorolf.

"Indirectly," the scribe said.

"I must know if a young woman came here last night."

This captured his attention. "Who is she?"

"Lady Runa—I am her servant."

The scribe waved the guards off and they lowered their weapons. "Join me, Sir. Your mistress has indeed been here."

Thorolf followed him through the sanctuary and another door which opened into the high priest's solar. He bowed to his lord.

"This man has requested a meeting with you, Master Hugin. He knows Lady Runa."

The priest looked up from his table, considered Thorolf for a moment, then addressed the scribe. "Leave us."

The servant bowed again, then left the room.

"Captain Thorolf?" Master Hugin poured a glass of wine and shoved the cup across the table. "I can see by your chains of office that you are the man Lady Runa was so worried about."

Thorolf picked up the cup and sniffed it before he dared to take a drink.

"I assure you there's no poison."

"Easily said if you've never been the target of such a thing." Thirsty, Thorolf gulped it down. "Where is Runa?" Under normal circumstances, he'd respect the formality expected in the temple. But there was no time to spare; he needed to find Runa.

"The lady is safe. She requested an armed escort back to the woods where she thought you might be. And the others…"

Thorolf made a sour face. "Sixteen men died at the hands of Jarl Skrymir. I narrowly escaped. I'm not even sure why he let me live."

Hugin's eyes widened. "The lady was telling the truth?"

Thorolf braced himself on the tabletop, spreading his hands wide, and leaned close to the priest. "You doubted her?"

The priest waved his fingers over the open flame of a candle burning in a holder nearby. "Do you know how many girls show up here every year begging for sanctuary? Weaving tales? Trying to avoid unwanted marriages?"

"Do they normally lie about a slaughter?"

Hugin sighed. "Never."

"Did she give you a reason to doubt her story?"

"No."

"Why did you send the guards with her? Wouldn't it have been easier to hold her here until you received word about what to do? She's the sister of one of the most powerful jarls in the Trondelag. Would it have not been more prudent to send word to him? To confirm her identity and purpose for being this far north without her family?"

The priest met his gaze. "I am well acquainted with *all* the chieftains in this part of our country. There are so few. We rely on the generosity of Prince Axel *and* Jarl Skrymir. The word of a lone girl against a man of Skrymir's reputation, though hostile as he's known to be, must be held in suspicion."

Thorolf muttered under his breath, then grabbed a fistful of the priest's tunic and hoisted him up. "Tis a matter of life and death. And that girl braved the dark and wilderness alone to get here, to find help for me and Prince Axel. And the loyal guards who perished for nothing." He shoved Hugin away. "Skrymir wanted the girl for himself. There's no other reason for what he did."

"Norway has seen its share of mad kings."

"Not murdering swine."

"Aye," the priest capitulated. "Tell me what I can do to help, Captain Thorolf."

"Send word to Jarl Roald."

"I will write the missive myself."

"Give me enough men to hunt Skrymir."

The priest rubbed his chin and stared at Thorolf long and

hard. "Where are you from, Captain?"

"Does my accent give me away?"

"Perhaps."

"Borg," he said.

"Yes. You are vaguely familiar to me…"

"No," Thorolf cut him off. "I've been gone for many years. I have no family left." Thorolf was determined to get what he wanted and snatched the flagon of wine off the table. He uncorked it and drank directly from the bottle, forgetting his manners. When he finished, he swiped the back of his hand across his mouth. "Enough small talk. Give me what I ask for."

"Gladly." Hugin smiled. "Just as soon as you pay for the first escort I sent out on your behalf."

"Where in Odin's ass did they find you?" Thorolf complained as he reached inside his tunic and pulled out a leather bag full of coins. "There's not a good man left in this country, is there?" He opened the purse and selected several gold pieces, then slammed them down on the table. "This will more than cover the loss of your guards."

The priest eyed the coins. "Yes, I believe it will." He stood and walked around the table, then opened the door. "Lonel, alert Captain Birger that he is needed at once." He closed the door and returned to his seat. "I will give you full command of twenty-five soldiers. In fact, you may keep them if you wish. With this much gold I can buy the loyalty of twice as many."

"I will report your unwavering dedication to Jarl Roald once I return home," Thorolf said coolly.

"Thank you, Captain. Feel free to use the temple as a staging point for your activities. There are several outbuildings reserved for guests who have business in the northlands. Captain Birger will show you."

Thorolf left the solar knowing this was no more a holy place than the pits in the ground outside where men squatted to shit. And though it disappointed him greatly, he didn't have time to care. In the future, though, he'd be sure to tell the high priest how wrong he thought he was.

Chapter Eighteen

GRANT ME PATIENCE. *Give me strength to endure this undeserved humiliation. I must remain obedient.* Olvir wanted to do the right thing. He'd spent years bending to his father's will, suffering to please him, to prove himself worthy as a son. But tonight, for a moment, he considered doing the impossible, standing up to his sire in front of his guards and guests.

The jarl was arguing with his captains about who had the steadiest hand with a bow after drinking six flagons of wine. A pile of silver coins had already accumulated on the table, the prize for whatever man proved himself the winner.

"What say you, my son?"

Olvir cleared his throat. "I have been gone too long to pick one from among these capable warriors."

"Spoken like a weakling," his father said. "I command you to choose. Will it be Knut? Rolf? Tristan?"

"None." Olvir stayed true to his word.

"Very well," the jarl said. "If you will not select a warrior, then you will become an important part of the contest."

He couldn't guess what his father wanted him to do. A target stuffed with straw had already been hung on the far wall. Instead of questioning it, he simply watched as the five participants lined up in the middle of the great hall, thirty paces from the target. The first round of the competition required each man to shoot his specially marked arrows in rapid succession. The arrows closest to the center ring would receive the most points.

The top three archers would advance to the next contest.

Once identified, a smaller target was hung on the wall. Again, the competitors did their best, but only two advanced to the final challenge.

Olvir had always admired Rolf the most. Though the man did his sire's bidding, as Olvir matured, the soldier often had kind words for him. Unlike the other warriors who taunted him as much as his father did. In fact, his sire encouraged them, hoping one day his son would prove everyone wrong. But Olvir knew that moment would never come.

The jarl stood and clapped his hands for Rolf and Knut. "Tis no surprise. Congratulations. Now for the final test." He gazed at Olvir, seated a couple chairs down. "Are you ready?"

Olvir dropped the piece of bread he was about to eat on his platter. "What will you have me do?"

"Bring in the squash!" Otkel said.

A thrall entered the great hall carrying the wintertime vegetable.

"Now give it to my son," his father ordered. "He will hold it while Rolf and Knut take a shot at it."

Olvir absolutely refused to do something so haphazard. One slip of a hand and he'd die. "Father..." He sucked down the last of his wine and stood. "I cannot do this."

The jarl grinned. "You can't do a lot of things, my son. And I've accepted your limitations, haven't I? Accommodated you? Tolerated your inferiority for years. I will not be denied, Olvir, so don't give me a reason to force you into submission. Now take the squash and go stand in front of the target. If I were capable of walking a straight line, I'd do it myself."

The remaining captains seated at the high table snickered.

"If you prefer it, Father, I will gladly walk you across the room."

Otkel cocked his head. "What do you fear? There is always blood at the end of these competitions we're all so fond of."

Olvir scrubbed his face with both hands, trying to wrap his mind around the twisted ways of his father. As long as someone else shouldered the risk, the jarl welcomed any form of entertainment. "Goodnight." He walked around the table and stepped off the dais, headed for his chamber.

Jarl Otkel slammed his fist on the table and shot up. "Tymon," he addressed a soldier sitting nearby. "Stop my son."

He immediately rose and glared at Olvir. "Listen to your sire, Boy. Don't force my hand."

Tymon gave him good counsel, but Olvir wasn't interested in the easiest solution. By God, he didn't wish to stay here another minute. He would gather what coinage he'd managed to save and leave the Trondelag forever, seeking passage on a ship bound for Northumbria. "Lay hands on a prince of Norway and you'll pay a heavy price." The empty threat slipped from his mouth before Olvir had a chance to really think before he spoke.

The hall went eerily silent then.

"A prince of Norway?" his father repeated incredulously. "You dare claim a title you've never earned or cared to defend?" Otkel staggered off the stage and walked toward his son. "Every man wearing a sword in this hallowed hall is more a prince than you'll ever be, ungrateful dog. Take up the position I've ordered you to."

Resolute, Olvir shook his head. "No."

The jarl's face twisted in anger as he spread his fingers wide and covered Olvir's face with his big hand, then gave him a violent shove.

Olvir stumbled back, his heart racing in fear. But he didn't fall down or cry out. Not this time. He'd never give his sire the satisfaction of seeing him run away again. Never. Even though his father was superior in size and strength, Olvir had gained confidence in his natural talents while serving Prince Ivarr in Northumbria. A brilliant mind could defeat the greatest of warriors.

"I will give you one chance to reconsider your choice," the jarl said.

"There is no need."

"Very well." Though twice his son's age, the jarl moved lethally quick and grabbed a fistful of his son's tunic and dragged him across the hall, to where the small target hung on the wall. "You will stand here and hold the vegetable high so my men can shoot at it. Do you understand?"

Olvir bucked against his father's brute strength, trying to twist free. It did no good. The jarl gave him a brain-rattling jolt.

"Obey me, Olvir." Otkel looked at the waiting thrall. "Bring it here. Now."

The jarl handed the squash to his son. "Hold it willingly or I will have the smithy bore a hole through it and hang it around your neck from a rope. Then we'll see what your chances of survival truly are."

Olvir's gaze darted nervously about the chamber, wondering who found this sort of torture entertaining. But from what he could see, no one looked especially comfortable. Not even the captains at the high table. Cowards all, really. None challenged his father. Not even Rolf. Knowing he had no choice, Olvir finally gave up.

"As you wish, Sir."

Otkel let go and smiled triumphantly. "Good boy. Choose whatever stance you wish, as long as the target is accessible to my men."

Olvir tested the weight of the squash as his father started to walk away. "Wait, Father."

"What now?"

"What if I wish to join in the game?"

The jarl rubbed his chin. "You wish to take up the bow?"

"Aye."

"Why?"

"Is this not the moment you've been waiting for?"

"Perhaps." His father considered it for a long moment. "If I give you this opportunity, what do I get in return?"

"Pride."

Otkel laughed. "A good answer. Very well. Rolf, give the boy a bow and let him take a couple practice shots at the small target before the final round of competition."

Olvir handed the vegetable to the thrall and waited for the captain to bring a weapon to him. Jarl Otkel returned to his throne and mead, looking more contented than he ever had.

Rolf approached with a somber expression on his face. "I am sorry for this."

"'Tis not your fault."

"Not directly," the captain said. "But if I'd intervened long ago, maybe things would be different between you and your father."

"A dozen sons wouldn't make my sire happy," Olvir said. "Nothing does. Not my mother, me, or even wealth and power."

"Aye."

"There is no need to stay close, Rolf, I am practiced enough on the bow. Even my soft hands were expected to practice occasionally while I was away."

The captain nodded and stepped aside as Olvir walked the distance to where the other men had stood to shoot. He then inspected the weapon. Made soundly, he positioned the bow properly, testing the string. Pleased with how it felt, he nocked an arrow and took aim at the small target, then released it. The arrow hit the center ring. Olvir did it again without pause.

The silence was broken by applause. But Olvir ignored the false praise and nocked another arrow. He'd taken the first two shots to impress his father, to demonstrate how wrong he'd been about his only son. Though Olvir preferred the duties of a scribe, he also recognized the importance of being able to defend himself and his home. Something he'd kept hidden, preferring to earn the respect of his people through what he loved to do most. He'd failed at it miserably.

Now he had no choice but to join in his father's madness.

Taking aim at the target again, he waited for his father to say something, anything.

"It seems my son has a streak of luck."

Without thinking, he whipped around, and released the arrow in the direction of his father. After it pierced him through the left eye socket, pinning his head to the back of his throne, for the first time in his twenty-three seasons, Olvir finally felt like the kind of man his father would admire.

Chapter Nineteen

RUNA DISMOUNTED AND joined the temple guards in the clearing where Prince Axel's camp had been. Nothing looked the same. Most of the tents had been dismantled. Bags were scattered everywhere, their contents littered the wet ground. The carefully constructed rock fire pits were broken up, appearing as if someone had tried to erase the evidence of who had been here before.

"There isn't a living creature about," one of the captains said somberly, shivering. "I am truly sorry for your loss, milady. Judging by the quick work of whoever attacked you, it isn't safe to stay here."

Runa wiped a stray tear from the corner of her eye. The memory of the threat and violence Jarl Skrymir presented had raised a fear inside her she'd never known. But standing here in the aftermath, seeing the destruction firsthand, conjured deep sorrow. No one appeared to have survived. As that realization started to sink in, another soldier called out.

"Over here, Captain Harald."

Runa started to follow him, but he stopped her. "Let me secure the area first."

"There's no need to shield me from blood and death. I've seen enough already." She scanned the field, finding bloodstains half-washed away by the rain. "I have as much right to see whatever it is your man has found."

"Aye," the captain agreed. "But will it serve any purpose? Make the outcome better? Cling to your hope and innocence as long as you can."

She appreciated his kind sentiment. "You have daughters?"

"Two."

"I understand your protectiveness, Sir. But I am the sister of Jarl Roald, a man who deals harshly with criminals. I've witnessed executions and numerous fights. Let us walk together."

He sucked in a breath and hesitantly took her arm. "The ground is rocky and uneven, let me help you."

His man waited across the clearing. No one needed to direct Runa where to look. Two dozen bodies were carefully stacked underneath protective layers of canvas. Confused by it, she blinked in disbelief. A cold-hearted murderer with a conscious? Skrymir surely hadn't wasted time gathering the dead. But someone had. "Captain—"

"You didn't exaggerate, lady. I am sorry if the high priest doubted your story."

"I expected no less," she said. "But now that we've confirmed everything, I am not sure we should leave yet. These men must be honored immediately, to keep their souls from getting trapped between worlds."

He bowed his head in acquiescence. "I am here to serve you."

"Ask your man to uncover the bodies. I wish to identify the men I knew."

Harald directed several of his soldiers to do as she bid. An hour later, the victims had been laid out on the ground. With grief in her heart, Runa walked slowly down three rows of bodies, pausing next to each one in respect. Giving thanks for their willingness to fight for and protect her. To die for Prince Axel.

She found her brother's men in the last row: Dain, Gudmund, and Isolf. It pained her to bid farewell to men she'd grown up around. She knelt beside Dain and caressed his brow. His eyes were closed, his cheeks pale and cold to the touch. "Forgive me," she whispered. "If it hadn't been for me, you'd still be in the Trondelag drinking your fill of mead."

Captain Harald stood on the other side of Dain. "Don't blame yourself, Lady. If these men were anything like the one's I lead, there's nothing else they'd rather do," he spoke in a fatherly tone.

She gazed up at him. "If you knew all the details, Captain, you might change your mind."

"Then offer a blood sacrifice to the gods on their behalf. No amount of crying and regret will bring them back. Don't mourn their deaths, celebrate their bravery."

It sounded right, but Runa was in no mood for merriment. Even to commemorate the slain. However, the idea of a blood sacrifice appealed to her. "Will you send a couple of your guards to hunt a stag?"

"At this time of day?" Harald peeked at the sun. "We'd have a better chance with rabbits or birds."

"No," she said adamantly. "Small creatures will not do."

"Twould be better to wait until evening or early morning."

Runa looked in the direction of the tethered horses. "If not a stag or wild boar, we will offer one of our horses."

"B-but..." Harald stumbled over his words. "We have none to spare."

She stood. "Whichever man is willing to donate his mount will be compensated three times the value of his horse." It felt good taking charge of the situation. Though it might take some work, Runa would convince the captain to agree to her demands.

"Very well. I will relay your offer to my men."

Hours later as the sun started to set, Runa stood in silence as she watched several soldiers with lit torches set fire to the five funeral pyres that had been constructed. The flames licked higher and higher, fueled by lamp oil found in one of the remaining tents. Beyond the pyres, the horse had already been killed, its blood poured over the burning bodies.

"Have you any words to offer, Lady Runa? Memories to share? Prayers to whisper?" Harald joined her.

"No. Tis better for me to hold my tongue."

"What wrong could a young woman have committed that she would blame herself for this slaughter?"

"No need to speak in generalities, Captain. I accept full responsibility."

"All right." He studied her. "What did you do?"

"I deceived my brother, Prince Axel, and all of these men by asking to visit the prince's home before I decided to marry him or not."

"You did nothing wrong."

"It was a way to avoid immediate marriage. I never intended to accept Axel's proposal. In doing so, I inadvertently opened these men up to Skrymir's attack."

"I see." Harald scratched his head and stared in the direction of the pyres. "Do you think you're the first girl to do such a thing? To covet freedom? To fight for a way to keep from marrying a man you don't know or want?"

"Tis nothing to trouble yourself about. I will carry this guilt with me forever, regardless of what you say to comfort me."

"But it is my concern." He gazed at her again. "I am a man of a different sort—forward thinking is the best way to describe it. And seeing as I will never sire sons, the gods gifted me with two daughters I refuse to raise as helpless creatures dependent on men alone for sustenance."

If only her brother possessed a fraction of this man's beliefs. "Thank you for your kindness."

Harald gestured toward the pyres. "If bones could talk, what do you think those men would say?"

For a while she said nothing, avoiding the thought. Somehow, Harald's sympathy and interest in her welfare made it impossible to ignore his question long term. That, and the fact he waited patiently next to her. "Perhaps they'd ask for mead. Or a chance to find Jarl Skrymir."

The captain chuckled. "All men love mead," he agreed. "As for Skrymir, I'm sure if given a choice between defending you or turning you over to the bastard to save themselves, they'd all choose to die again. The outside world has unfairly judged Norsemen out of fear. Though we seek death in glorious battle, we never abandon honor. Women must be protected from the evils in this world."

"But unnecessary death..."

"The gods decide the time of a man's death. If not this way, then another."

Could she accept this explanation? If so, she might find inner peace again someday. But for now, a violent storm of regret and guilt raged inside her. "Will we search for Captain Thorolf and Prince Axel's bodies in the morning?"

Harald's grim face suggested otherwise. "Aye, we can sweep the surrounding forest, but I am not sure we will find anything. Hungry beasts are everywhere."

Runa sank to the ground then, tears sliding down her cheeks. The idea of a bear dragging Thorolf's body off made her sick—made her want to curl into a little ball and die. "Every effort must be made to recover them."

"Aye."

"Now, please..." She dried her eyes on her sleeve. "Leave me to mourn the loss of these men alone."

Harald bowed and walked away.

She stared at the dancing flames, wondering what she would do if she were given the chance to see Captain Thorolf a last time. What would she say to him? Do with him? "I'd say I love you," she whispered. "Again and again so you'd never forget it. Then I'd stare at you endlessly, because I've never met a more beautiful man. Nor a more honorable one. Now I must learn to live without you, Thorolf. Odin help me, I won't let your death be in vain."

More than ever, Runa wanted to serve in the temple, where her maidenhood would be safeguarded from the world of common men. Where she'd live out her life remembering the past and hoping to prove herself worthy of Allfather's favor.

Chapter Twenty

THOROLF AND HIS new guards surrounded the clearing where his camp had been in the middle of the night. Several fires burned in the clearing, a handful of soldiers kept watch, but not enough to win a fight if Thorolf ordered an attack.

"Captain Birger," he motioned for the eldest of the soldiers to join him. "The high priest said Lady Runa and the regiment escorting her might come here. Before we launch an offensive, go and see if you recognize any of the soldiers in the camp. Raise your left hand if you do, the right if you don't."

"Aye," the captain said.

"If your right hand, be prepared for the assault."

Fifteen of the twenty-five guards were positioned on the far side of the clearing, waiting for the signal to move—a raven call made three times. The remaining ten were with Thorolf. Not taking his eyes off Birger, the man walked casually to the central campfire and gripped the forearm of one of the watchmen.

Thorolf took a relieved breath, knowing the captain, indeed, knew the man. Then Birger raised his left hand.

"Stand down," Thorolf ordered. "One of you go and inform the others. There will be no bloodshed tonight."

The hardest part should be over. But in all reality, it wasn't. Not for him. Because somewhere in the midst of the handful of tents set up, Lady Runa awaited him. Or mourned him. Whichever didn't matter. They must speak at once. And after fearing for her life over the last day and night, he wasn't sure he could ever let her marry another man, even if it was Prince Axel. He walked across the clearing to where Birger waited.

"Captain Thorolf," Birger said, "This is Tage, the man in charge of the night watch."

Thorolf acknowledged the soldier. "Where is your superior?"

"Asleep, Sir."

"And Lady Runa?"

The warrior eyed him suspiciously then. "I was given specific orders. No one is to disturb her. She's in deep mourning."

"I understand," Thorolf said. "Much life was lost here. Good men. But I assure you, the lady will want to see me."

Birger whispered something to Tage and then the younger man's features lit up.

"You are *the* Captain Thorolf she weeps for?"

"Aye."

"By everything sacred," he said in awe and pointed toward an area sheltered on three sides by trees. "She occupies that lone tent."

A part of Thorolf wanted to scream her name and go running to the tent. But logic overruled his unravelling emotions. He'd spent too many years denying himself pleasure—beating down the feelings that made any warrior a real man. Not just flesh and blood, but heart.

"Do you have any mead? Wine?" Thorolf asked.

"Yes." Tage hurried a few feet away to where he'd been sitting and picked up a wineskin. He brought it back to Thorolf. "Take mine."

Grateful, Thorolf uncorked it and took a generous swig.

"Has the lady eaten anything?"

"No," Tage answered. "Captain Harald is concerned about her lack of appetite."

"Give me some bread. I will convince her to eat." Thorolf turned to Birger. "Keep watch with this capable soldier. Encourage the others to rest. I'll see you in the morning."

"Aye," Birger bowed.

Carrying a sack of bread and the wineskin, Thorolf slowly made his way to Runa's shelter. He paused outside the opening to listen for any noise. Nothing. And there was no light visible along the seams of the flap. Perhaps she'd fallen asleep. No matter, nothing would keep him from laying eyes on her.

He stepped inside, finding a single candle lit on a crate in the corner. The sound of steady breathing calmed his nerves, for he needed to see and hear she was all right, really alive. He dropped the bread and wineskin on the ground and approached her pallet. Curled on her left side, facing away from him, wisps of dark hair covered her face. He reached for her cheek, gently moving the curls out of the way. Her pale skin glimmered in the candlelight, flawless and so temptingly touchable. Kissable.

Kneeling beside her, Thorolf watched in fascination. How could any woman get more beautiful? Only Runa.

"I am here, pretty one," he whispered. "Shed no more tears for me. Banish the nightmares. Stop blaming yourself for taking my counsel to heart. Blame me for your misfortune."

Unable to resist the need to make contact with her soft-looking flesh, he brushed her cheek with the back of his hand, closing his eyes as he did. He flinched. Love and lust shot through him, mingling, and robbing him of logic. "One touch always leads to another."

He retreated, fearing the effect of a second touch.

"You're a ghost to me," he murmured as he helped himself

to another measure of mead. "You haunted me, Lady. Made it impossible to sleep. I feared for your life at the hands of Skrymir. But I promise you this, Lady Runa…"

He paused as she stirred and rolled onto her back.

"Skrymir will die for what he's done. And if I fail to deliver his head to you, then I will die for not keeping this oath." He unsheathed his knife and dragged it across his palm. "My blood seals this promise between me, you, and the gods."

"Captain Thorolf?" her soft voice sounded. "Tell me I'm not dreaming."

Thorolf looked up and found Runa on her hands and knees, staring at him.

"Tell me, now," she demanded.

"This is no dream. I am here."

She cried out. "Odin saved you." Tears streamed down her cheeks. "Prince Axel told me to run. I didn't want to leave you, Thorolf. Please forgive my cowardice. I-I…"

"Cowardice?" He jumped to his feet, angry she'd ever consider herself weak. "You are just the opposite, Lady."

"Skrymir poisoned most of the men. Others were put to the sword. We cremated the bodies as soon as we got here, Thorolf. Someone moved them…"

"Twas me." He took a step closer.

"How did you escape?"

"I didn't. I woke in pain, remembering the jarl kicking me in the ribs and that someone bashed me in the back of the head. Twice I think." He rubbed the back of his skull, the sizable lump reminding him of his near lethal mistake. "I must beg your forgiveness, Lady Runa."

"F-for what?" Her eyes grew wide.

"I let jealousy blind me for the first time in my life." He held her questioning gaze as he dropped to his knees before her.

"There is no excuse for my behavior." He bowed his head in submission, as any soldier must do if he failed his master. "Punish me as you see fit."

A little out of breath, she kneeled before him, lifting his chin. Their gazes met and he couldn't help but admire the deep green of her eyes. "Tis I who must beg forgiveness, Captain Thorolf. I lied to my family, manipulated the good prince, and flaunted everything in front of you without a care for how you felt."

"And how do I feel, Lady?"

She adverted her eyes, staring at the floor. "I believe you love me, Thorolf."

As soon as she'd spoken those words, something broke inside him. He gathered her in his arms and lifted her to her feet. "Do you know what you say?"

"Do you?" Her hands started to shake.

By the gods… She welcomed his love? Wanted it? "Do not toy with my heart, Runa. I am nothing like the men your brother summoned to the Trondelag. I won't tolerate you flirting with another man. Or pretending to love one."

She stiffened. "Is that a threat?"

"Only truth."

"Thorolf…"

No more words were needed. He'd grown tired of waiting and tugged her into his arms, cradling her warm, soft body against his. Her sweet scent danced around him, feeding his need to possess her. Those lips. Her fathomless eyes. The feel of her tiny hands on his arms. He slanted his mouth over hers, forcing her lips open with his tongue, tasting what he'd considered his all along. Enjoying the velvety feel of her tongue sliding over his, tangling his heart in a web of lust and love.

The forbidden had been taken. The untouchable, caressed a thousand times in his thoughts and dreams. To Hel with Jarl

Roald, Prince Axel, Jarl Skrymir, and any other man that would dare lay claim to her.

Lady Runa belonged to him now.

He pushed her away then, needing to put some distance between them before he did something they'd both regret later. But her heated look said something different. Thorolf recognized deep hunger when he saw it.

"Why did you stop?" she demanded.

He rubbed his chin, eyeing her kiss-swollen lips—proof of where he'd been seconds earlier. Then his gaze dipped lower, naturally drawn to the outline of her pebble-hard nipples protruding through the thin material of her shift. Not noticing her state of undress before, he realized even her ankles and small feet were visible. Slim ankles at that.

"Stop ogling me like a hungry dog, Captain Thorolf, and tell me how you feel."

"I'd rather show you," he growled, circling her. "Haven't enough men told you pretty lies? Begged for your heart?"

"Remember your place, Captain," she said, her confidence restored.

"And where is that, Lady Runa?"

She folded her hands over her stomach, then released them, only to do it again.

"Have you no answer?"

"I can't think clearly with you staring at me so intensely."

"Tell me my place." He tipped her chin, admiring the haughty look on her pretty face.

"I-I..."

"Shall I help you, Lady, by telling you where *you* belong?" His body begged for relief.

"Aye."

Thorolf rewarded her with a wicked grin and swept her off

her feet as she gasped in shock. "Beneath me, Runa. That's where you belong, now and forever." He carried her to the narrow mattress on the ground and spread her out.

He unfastened his sword belt, letting it fall on the ground, then stripped his clothes and boots off with a fury he'd never known. Lowering himself gently on top of her, he lifted her arms above her head, once again claiming that sharp tongue with his mouth. He'd give her every reason to love and respect him, to call him lord. To reject every other man that came her way.

She shifted underneath him, spreading her legs wide enough for his body to fit comfortably between them. The only thing stopping him from sinking deep inside her was the linen shift she wore. *Miserable little piece of cloth.* Still holding her wrists in place above her head with one hand, he reached for the laces on her bodice. With a rough tug, he snapped the leather string and the material sagged open, revealing the generous curves of her full breasts.

Runa sucked in a breath, then arched her spine in welcome. "Kiss me."

"Aye," he said. "I will do more than that." He released her hands and slid down her body, level with her chest. Opening the top of her shift more, a pert breast popped out and he caught the nipple between his teeth and nibbled and licked it. "You are perfect in every way," he praised her, his cock ready to burst. "And mine now…"

She dug her fingernails into the sides of his head, squirming and begging. "Please," she panted. "Touch me all over."

Thorolf started at her toes, tasting and caressing every inch of her flesh, lifting the hem of her shift above her thighs as he climbed higher and higher. Until both of her beautiful breasts were exposed and cradled in his palms.

"The spot between my legs is throbbing," she said. "Why?"

With care, Thorolf slipped two fingers inside her core, greeted by wet heat. He gritted his teeth as he slid in and out, silently willing her to come. "The first lesson of many," he said, burying his face between her luscious thighs, loving the feel of her soft nest of black curls rubbing against his chin.

Within seconds she went rigid, the pulse of her satisfaction against his tongue, proof enough that he could please her body and, one day, rule her heart.

Chapter Twenty-One

ENVELOPED IN THOROLF'S strong embrace, Runa wondered why he'd done everything to her but the final act that made a man and woman one. She'd been too nervous to ask just after he finished showing her how to caress his manhood properly. And it slipped her mind as she explored his perfectly muscled body with her hands and tongue, trying to mimic the pleasurable caresses and nibbles he'd done to her. Proud she'd only made him wince in pain once as she bit his thigh too hard, the real satisfaction came when he released his seed in her hands.

"Go to sleep, Runa," he said. "There is much to be done in the morning."

"How can I sleep after what we shared?"

He flipped her onto her back and balanced himself on his elbows. "I won't despoil you for a night of passion, Runa. It goes against everything I believe in, the way I live my life."

"Shouldn't I be the one to decide?" Despite bold words, she could feel the flush creeping up her cheeks.

"What experience do you have in the ways of sex and love?"

She clicked her tongue. "I have a heart, don't I?"

"Aye, there is that."

"Then why deny me the chance to give you my most precious gift?"

Thorolf repositioned himself on his side, resting his head against his palm. He fingered a long strand of her hair. "Your brother will try to kill me once he discovers our relationship."

She sat up, shaking her head. "I won't let him."

"Listen to me, Runa. He entrusted me with your life. Instead of delivering you safely to Prince Axel's home, we were attacked, our men killed, and now I've bedded you—well, almost bedded you. Undeniable betrayal."

"You sound as if you regret it." It pained her to think so, because she'd given Thorolf everything she had inside her a few hours ago. Her fingers had become an extension of her heart once she began touching and kissing him.

He entwined his fingers with hers and lifted her hand to his mouth, kissing it. "Never. How can you even suggest it, Lady?"

"Because your words and actions do not match. I felt your love, but I cannot see it. You still haven't told me how you feel."

He sighed and released her hand. "Do you think it's easy for a man to speak from the heart? I'd rather face Thor on the battlefield."

"Then let me."

"No." He held a finger to her lips to shush her.

"So you'd even rob me of the right to confess my love?"

"I'd not have you admit to anything you'd soon regret. I am a man without a home. No lands. No family. No title. What kind of husband will I be? Not the sort your brother will ever approve of."

Runa crossed her arms over her chest, still confused by the sudden change in Thorolf's attitude. "I care nothing for wealth. I'd rather have your mind and heart. Your love, Captain Thorolf. I adore and love you." There, she'd said it.

A distant look darkened his features then.

"It is too late to worry about your lack of a title, Thorolf.

How could I ever give myself to another man after what we've done?"

"Another man will *never* have you, Runa. Not as long as there is breath left in my body. Or faith in the gods in my heart. You want to hear love words from a broken man? I will speak the truth, always. I've loved you from the first day we met in the great hall. Though I thought you self-indulgent and unmanageable, I wanted to be near you, to see the flames of passion in your eyes. That's how you know someone is truly alive. And you, above all others, are truly alive. Even now, suffering from the guilt and loss of those men, the fire burns even brighter inside you. Heat radiates from your tiny body like it does from the sun."

Her mouth dropped open.

"Yes, Runa. I want you to wife. To be the mother of my children. I love you." He sat up and pulled her into the most intimate hug.

In his arms, nothing could harm her. Even Roald seemed too far away to influence her life. Thorolf might not possess lands or great wealth, but he owned Runa's heart. Together, they could carve out their own future, perhaps purchase enough land to farm and comfortably support a family. She had gold and silver saved, gifts from her mother and a small inheritance from her father.

"Listen to me, Lady." Thorolf held her away from his body. "There's grave danger everywhere right now. Skrymir didn't slaughter these men for nothing. He wants you, I'm sure of it. If he finds out about us, he'll use our love as a weapon against us. We must keep our feelings secret for now. Until I've captured and killed the bastard. Then I will go to your brother and ask for your hand in marriage."

"I don't want to hide from the world, Thorolf."

"Only for a short time. I promise."

She nodded, reluctant to agree, but left with no choice. Thorolf wasn't the kind of man to be denied. "How many children do you want?" she asked, hoping to lighten the mood.

"Not as many as Prince Axel," he teased.

Dear gods ... the man's mother bore fifteen babes and had survived. "Thank you for your consideration."

He chuckled. "Four or five will do nicely."

"If that is the case, Sir, shouldn't you show me how children are made?"

His brows shot up. "You really don't know?"

"I have an idea, but have never confirmed it."

He raked his fingers through his shoulder-length blond hair. "You know how to push a man beyond his limits, Runa."

She shot an admiring look between his legs, his manhood standing at full attention again. Had it ever stopped? The sight of it, how firm and thick it was, knowing even if she lined her two hands up along its length, it wasn't enough to contain him. And that was supposed to fit inside her? She shivered.

"Runa?"

She peeked up at him.

"You know more than you wish to tell."

She shook her head. "Just what I dream of with you."

He growled at her words, propelling closer to her. "Do you need another lesson?"

"I need you."

With no warning, he lifted her onto his stomach as he laid back on the pallet. "Straddle me, Runa. Get on all fours and slide upward, until your center is hovering above my mouth."

She froze, stuck inside her imagination trying to picture the position he wanted her to get in. What did he intend to do with her? The possibilities were endless. Wetness pooled between her thighs and that dull ache had returned.

"Runa?"

She did as he asked, determined to please him in every way.

Rocking forward on her elbows, arse bobbing in the air, Thorolf gripped her thighs and urged her lower. She cried out as his tongue slipped between her slick folds, followed by his fingers. *Odin have mercy…* His tongue circled over her hard nub. Sensations shot up her spine, almost too intense to enjoy. But then he did something incredible with his fingers that eased the feeling and brought her spiraling down, into a more comfortable place.

She rode his face like a longship on ocean waves, rolling her hips over him until his tongue triggered that endless pulsing that made her lose her breath and scream out his name.

After, she lay motionless on top of him, wishing for more.

"There are many things we can do without sacrificing your maidenhead before we are wed."

Those *many things* seemed to favor her more than him. "I want to make you happy, too, Thorolf. Don't you need to be touched like I do?"

"Captain Thorolf?"

Runa scrambled off Thorolf, searching for a loose fur to cover herself with. The captain jumped up, roaring in anger.

"Did I invite you inside this tent, Birger?"

The man looked at Thorolf first, then his gaze wandered to Runa.

"Turn around, Captain Birger," Thorolf commanded, unashamed of his nakedness. "Walk out of this shelter and forget what you saw. I will join you momentarily."

"Aye." Birger departed with haste.

Thorolf turned to Runa. She'd managed to pull a fur about her shoulders, but knew the stranger had seen too much of her.

"Who is he?"

"One of the soldiers the high priest sold to me."

"A thrall?"

"No. A sell-sword."

"Can he be trusted?"

"As much as the next man with no chieftain or home." Thorolf closed the distance between them, cupped her face between both hands, and kissed her forehead tenderly. "Don't worry, Lady. If he talks, I'll carve his tongue out. Now bathe and dress. I will send a guard to accompany you to the fire. We must decide what our next move is."

"Can we go home?"

He shook his head. "No. I don't want to endanger anyone unnecessarily. I've secured quarters for us at the temple. You'll be safe."

"How long do we have to stay away from the Trondelag?" she asked.

"As long as it takes to rid the world of Jarl Skrymir and claim his mountain stronghold as my own."

Chapter Twenty-Two

AFTER OLVIR SHOT his father in the eye with an arrow, he fled the great hall and sought refuge in the forest. No one tried to stop his escape, in fact, no one reacted to his actions whatsoever. Maybe shock had silenced the usually capable guards and smug guests his sire surrounded himself with. It didn't matter anymore. Jarl Otkel was dead.

"I am a wanted man now, Rolf. Surely there's a bounty on my head already," Olvir said. Only a fool committed murder in front of fifty people.

Rolf poked at the dwindling campfire with a stick, mixing the ashes and kindling like stew. "Account for your actions, Boy. Don't run away, it only makes you look guilty."

Olvir didn't understand why his father's favorite captain had followed him into the wilderness. Appreciative of the man's company, he wrestled with the need to ask. "Go back, Rolf, don't risk your life by staying with me."

"Do you know how long I waited for you to challenge your father? To end the continuous humiliation you suffered at his hands? I can scarce blame you for killing him. Nor will anyone who witnessed it."

"It was not an honorable course."

"Perhaps not," the captain said. "But brave for the boy I've known."

Ashamed, Olvir stared at the ground. "If you haven't noticed, I am no longer a boy."

"Until last night you were."

He raised his head. "My age says different."

Rolf tapped his right temple with his fingers. "The body matters little if the mind lags behind."

"You speak like a scholar, not a warrior."

"I spent more time listening as a youth. I wield ax and sword for a living. There are a hundred men to replace me if I fall. But how many men can read and write? Speak as many languages as you? Negotiate with strangers and make peace? You are meant to take your rightful place as the next jarl."

"I've been the butt of my father's cruel jokes for too long. His men contributed to my misery. Laughing at me, beating me, questioning my manhood at every turn. You are the only exception, Rolf. How can you expect me to return and ask those same men to pledge allegiance to me? To let me rule over them. I can't even win the bride I want. She was smart enough to recognize the fool I am years ago. My only choice is to seek sanctuary at the temple and make arrangements to return to Northumbria."

Suddenly Olvir regretted not living by the sword. The written word couldn't save a man's life like a sharp ax and strong arm. "I am not worthy of my father's title. Nor do I want it."

"Truly?" Rolf stood. "You'd let your family legacy disappear with your sire? You prefer living outside like an animal over the comfort of your home?"

"I believe I have some distant cousins somewhere in this country. Let power be transferred to that line of my family."

Rolf rejected his suggestion with a wave of his hand. "The gods will choose the next jarl, not you."

"Maybe," he said with a shrug. "I'd still rather take my

chances with the high priest. Besides, I have no dedicated protectors. If I show my face again, someone will kill me to avenge my father."

The captain patted the hilt of his sword. "And what do you think I am?"

"I don't know, Captain. A bigger dolt than I?"

Rolf chuckled. "Give me the wineskin."

Olvir gladly turned it over to his only friend in the world. "What I would give to relive the past." Memories of his mother filled his mind then. Thank God it was dark amongst the trees. Rolf would never see the tears in his eyes. "I'd pay closer attention to my good teachers. Especially the master swordsman."

"Despite the pain?" Rolf questioned. "Do you recall how many times I lifted you out of the dust because you were angry at the pain you had to endure at swordplay? I've never seen a boy get so mad."

Olvir let himself smile. "Yes, I'd even accept the pain."

"And what of the girl you love?"

"Lady Runa?" Her silky dark hair and green eyes were unforgettable. "I'd be the man she deserved."

The captain stomped over to where he sat and gripped Olvir by the collar, slowly lifting him to his feet. Olvir had no choice but to meet his gaze. "Listen to me. The longer you stay away, the easier it will be for someone to usurp power. The sooner you press your right to the seat, the better your chances at winning your bride. A man with a title, lands, and power usually gets what he wants." He gave Olvir a little shake before he let go of his tunic.

Could he dare dream of such a life? They'd call him Jarl Olvir. But his name reminded him too much of his father. Should he change it to something more impressive? Jarl Agdon?

Or Jarl Haakon? The true reward would be taking Runa to wife. Their children would be beautiful. Strong. Intelligent. Sought after. "Stop filling my head with nonsense, Rolf. I command you to eat and drink your fill, then to get on your horse and ride back to the Trondelag. Tell whoever asks, you could not find me. No one will doubt your word."

"Forgive me, milord." Captain Rolf knelt in front of him. "This one time I must disobey a direct order. But from this moment onward, I pledge my sword and life to you. *Jarl Olvir.*"

The grim reality of Olvir's deed was forgotten as this celebrated warrior knelt before him, offering to serve him, to give his life in exchange for Olvir's headship. He tentatively reached for the captain's head. But before he touched it, his hand shook uncontrollably. "You mistake me for a lord, Rolf. Get up."

The captain didn't speak or move.

"If I only had half your strength and courage..." Olvir observed as he finally laid his hand on Rolf's head. The man's loyalty inspired Olvir, gave him renewed hope in himself and the possibility that he might make a fair jarl. "I accept your fealty, Rolf the Gray. No man has served my family better and no man ever will. Help me keep my jarldom and I will make you a rich man."

Chapter Twenty-Three

A MESSENGER HAD ARRIVED in the middle of the night, forcing the captain of the night watch to wake Jarl Roald and his wife. From there, everything went downhill. Though Runa had survived an attack by Jarl Skrymir, many were dead. Thorolf had been injured. And Prince Axel was missing—likely left in the woods to rot.

"Nothing will quell my rage, Eva. Nothing."

She held their infant son to her breast, trying to quiet him. As for his twin sister, she could sleep through anything. "I caution you to think clearly before you act my beloved husband," she warned. "Your temper..."

"Is justified in this situation."

"Yes," she said. "Completely. But remember how deservedly you dealt with my brother once your anger subsided some. Instead of taking his life..."

"Skrymir is a different matter altogether," he said darkly, trying to control the tone of his voice. Eva had been nothing but a source of excellent advice. "There are no blood ties with this man. No obligations. I see this attack as a declaration of war. I will break him." He pounded his fist against his palm. "I welcomed that bastard into our home."

Eva placed their son in his basket next to the bed, then joined Roald by the table. She cradled his hand in hers. "I think you are missing the most important thing."

"What?"

"Runa and Captain Thorolf are alive and safe."

"Alive, yes. Safe?" He didn't believe it. Not with Skrymir roaming freely in the northlands, having the advantage of being so close to his home. "It seems my sister's wish has been granted."

Eva gave him a sideways look.

"The temple," he pointed out, irritated. "She made it to the bloody temple after all."

"Not by choice."

"Maybe not. But I swear the girl conspired with Odin himself."

"I am sure the last thing on Runa's mind is swearing the oath of a temple maiden."

Roald laughed. "After everything she's been through? How can I convince the girl marriage is an honorable pursuit after she almost got killed for visiting the home of a prospective husband? Even if she lied to us about it."

Someone knocked on the door.

"Enter," Roald called.

Konal stood in the entryway, an ominous expression on his face. "Let me lead the guards northward. I will bring our sister home."

"No. I will go myself. I expect you to stay here and protect our holdings. Preserve our family. If anything happens to me, you will become jarl until my son comes of age."

"Goddamnit, Roald." Konal crossed the threshold and slammed the door shut. "What interest do you have in Runa beyond seeing her advantageously wed?"

"Don't question me in front of my wife."

Konal puffed out his chest. "Don't pretend to love our sister suddenly."

Eva looked between them. "Stop it at once. Konal, don't ever doubt my husband's tender feelings for your sister. Though they agree on nothing, he loves her. And as for you..." She turned to Roald. "You'll have no one left to serve you if you treat them so harshly."

Roald swallowed the lump in his throat. "I need you stay here and look after our families. There's no one I trust more."

His brother's shoulders relaxed some. "Promise me you'll deal gently with Runa."

"You have my word."

"Thank you."

"Another thing," Roald started. "Assemble the men while I ready for the journey."

Konal didn't answer, but left with urgency.

Eva sat on the end of the bed and covered her face with both hands. Roald couldn't ignore the sniffling sound she made and went to her side. Tipping her chin upward, he saw the tears in her eyes.

"Why do you weep?"

"For you. Our children. Runa and Thorolf."

"But we are well, Eva."

"Are we?" She pulled her knees under her chin. "Well? Or just existing?"

"Now isn't the time for a philosophical discussion."

"Why not?"

"Are the spirits talking to you again?"

"They never cease," she informed him.

He scratched his chin. "What say them now?" he asked, walking to his trunk and selecting his thickest braies. Full armor was required for this quest. "Dire warning? Words of wisdom for a brash Viking who wants to spill blood?"

"Spill blood, Jarl Roald," she said in that voice too familiar to him when the spirits possessed his wife's mind. "Only, spill the *right* blood."

Those words stopped him short and he spun around. "Explain yourself."

Eva rubbed her eyes, then stared at him blankly. "Explain what, my love?"

Unsure he'd ever adjust to her episodes, he smiled. "Nothing, Eva. Go back to sleep." He focused on getting dressed again, swearing by the nine realms that he'd secure his sister, reward Thorolf for his dedication, and destroy Skrymir, even if it meant dying.

RUNA COULDN'T BELIEVE the extent of the temple complex and how many people it took to run it. Captain Harald had volunteered to be her bodyguard as long as she stayed here and was giving her a tour of the grounds.

"A thousand people live here?" she asked, admiring the women working in the weaving room, twenty looms in use.

"Aye," he answered proudly. "The wool and tapestries made here help finance the rest of our operations. The northern lords generously donated the lands we occupy, giving us the freedom to act as an independent kingdom. The high priest and the council are the authority in this place, Lady. Much like your brother, Jarl Roald, they appoint men and women to run various ventures that benefit our people."

"I never knew."

"My very home is on the edge of these lands, the place I will retire to in a few years."

"Do you own the property?"

"In almost every sense of the word, though I don't hold a

deed."

"How many northern jarls are there?" she inquired as the captain escorted her to the dye room, where a dozen women were busily mixing vats of purple and green tinctures with long paddles.

"Sixteen."

"I'm afraid that number has shrunk."

"Yes," Harald agreed. "Unless we find Prince Axel alive and well, we will only have fourteen."

"I am sure my brother has been generous with your cause."

"The Trondelag is a thriving region," he said. "Home to some of the greatest warriors. Many of our guards come from there. As for silver and gold, I know little of who fills the great priest's coffers."

"But they *are* full." How couldn't it be so? Though a quarter of the size of her home, the accommodations here, the smoke-houses, storerooms, even the bathhouse, were more lavish than anything she'd ever seen. "May we visit the maidens next?"

Harald cleared his throat, looking suddenly uncomfortable. "Outsiders aren't permitted in their quarters."

"What do you mean? Men? That I understand. But surely a woman..."

The captain pulled her out of the dye house and away from anyone who might overhear him. "Yes, women of good reputation are encouraged to visit the temple maidens whenever possible. The priests rely on their positive reports to encourage the next generation of girls to come here. However..." He looked about before he continued. "This must stay between us, Lady Runa."

"Of course." He'd piqued her curiosity.

"Captain Thorolf forbade me from taking you there. He mentioned something about a childhood obsession and swore if

I didn't keep you away, he'd cut off any support for this place."

Runa's hands went to her hips, utterly disgusted by Thorolf's exaggeration. "Such impertinence cannot be tolerated."

"Perhaps you'd like to visit the stables next?"

"Why should I care about horses when I can visit the virtuous women who serve Allfather unfailingly?"

"Please," Harald pleaded. "I gave my solemn oath. Captain Thorolf doesn't strike me as the kind of man to forgive anything too quickly."

Runa stared off in the distance, admiring the creek that meandered through the property, providing fresh water and a pretty place to sit underneath the many trees. She must convince Harald to help her. "Midday is upon us, Captain. Aren't you accustomed to breaking bread now? If you'll point me in the right direction, we can part, and I will find my own way to the maidens."

Harald scratched at the side of his nose, thinking. "The captain was right about one thing."

"Oh?"

"He warned me about your craftiness, Lady. But how could I deny you? You remind me too much of my own daughters."

Runa smiled at the compliment. "I'd like to meet them later."

"An honor we'd never forget," he said kindly. "Follow the footpath northward. Around the altar stones on the side of the temple. Yards away you'll find a freestanding stone house. Odin's daughters live there."

Overjoyed by the captain's willingness to aid her, she stood on her toes and planted a friendly kiss on his cheek. "May the gods bless you, Captain Harald." Then she departed, eager to meet the maidens.

Chapter Twenty-Four

THE BETTER PART of the day had been spent searching tirelessly east of the temple for any traces of Skrymir. By the time the pale winter sun had started to fade, Thorolf remembered what day it was. The first full moon of the month, making it a sacred feast night—Thurseblot—in honor of Midgard's great protector, Thor. He rode hard through the snow to reach the temple grounds and find Runa.

Distracted by the events of the last week, Thorolf wouldn't miss a chance to celebrate with Runa. Having been to the temple as a boy to celebrate this very holiday, he could recall every detail. Runa would enjoy it.

As he trotted closer to the stables, he spotted Runa and Captain Harald through the trees. They seemed to be engaged in an animated conversation. Thorolf dismounted and parted the branches of the closest pine to get a better look. He huffed out a misted breath, wondering why the captain had pointed toward the temple. What he saw next made him suspicious. Runa kissed Harald's cheek and ambled away, looking happy—too happy for comfort.

He tied his mount to a nearby post and followed Runa. Then it hit him. The girl had worked her magic on the captain. She was headed for the cottage where the maidens were housed. Something he'd made Harald swear to keep Runa from doing.

Damn her ability to talk a man into doing whatever she wanted.

Able to take a shortcut through the trees, he blocked her way up the hill and waited for her to catch up.

When she finally did, he didn't miss the iciness of her stare. "Are you following me, Captain?"

Thorolf held back his laughter and gave her a mock bow. "Up this hill for sure."

Her tiny hands fisted at her sides, a clear indication she didn't appreciate the humor in his answer. "Y-you know what I meant."

"I just returned from the east woods, another failed attempt at finding a trace of Skrymir or Prince Axel."

"I am sorry to hear it."

"As am I," he said. "I returned as quickly as I could, Lady. I wanted to invite you to sit with me at the feast tonight."

"Feast?"

"Tis Thurseblot."

Looking bewildered, she said, "Dear Odin, how could I forget something so important?"

"I could brave a guess if you'd like."

"Brave a guess? As if I could stop you, Thorolf."

He loved the spark in her eyes whenever she got mad at him. His braies were suddenly too tight in the crotch area. "Perhaps you were too preoccupied kissing another man to think clearly."

"W-what?"

"Your good captain looked pleased with himself."

Sputtering, Runa came at him and slapped his chest with both hands. "You wretched beast."

Convulsing with laughter, he caught her hands and gave her a tiny shake. "How many times do I have to tell you those beautiful lips belong to me?" He hauled her close and captured her pouty lower lip between his teeth. Then skillfully filled her mouth with his tongue, silencing her instantly.

It pleased him when she melted against him, not struggling to get away, but kissing him with equal passion. Raw emotions exploded inside him, his body demanding more of her—preferably naked and in his bed. He could kiss her for hours but... "We must be careful," he warned, withdrawing. "Remember, even the trees have eyes and ears."

Her face had turned a lovely shade of pink. "The trees in the Trondelag suffer from the same malformation, I think."

Good, her sense of humor was still intact. "I won't let your kisses keep me from getting the answers I deserve, Runa. Now tell me, why are you headed up this hill? And why did you kiss the captain? Have I neglected you so much that you wish to replace me already?"

She frowned and he pinched her cheek playfully.

"The captain is old enough to be my father."

Thorolf shrugged. "Some women prefer the experience of an older man."

"Your teasing grows tedious, Sir."

"Does it?"

"Besides, you already know the answer. I want to meet the maidens."

"So the captain betrayed my trust?"

"Don't be ridiculous."

Thorolf leaned closer and whispered in her ear, "I hate to disappoint you, but I'm certain those lovely women aren't maidens anymore."

She pushed him away, annoyed. "Do tell, Thorolf. I am sure you had nothing to do with despoiling them. For as much as I don't wish it, I am stuck being a virgin." Her eyelashes fluttered appealingly.

The little minx.

"Step aside, Captain. I wish to visit the temple maidens."

Realizing he'd never be able to stop her, he offered his arm. "I will escort you myself."

HOURS AFTER HER VISIT with Odin's daughters, Runa prepared for the feast honoring Thor. Assigned a maid by the high priest, the girl worked diligently on her hair, spiraling thin strands around a wire circle, then pinning it in place. The front and the sides of her head were decorated in this way, the rest of her hair cascaded down her back.

Runa was grateful Thorolf had recovered two of her four bags from the camp. One of them contained her best gowns. She'd chosen a sky blue silk for the celebration, cut demurely in the bodice, but it dipped low enough to show a hint of cleavage. Once the servant had finished with her hair and jewelry, she offered Runa a small mirror.

"You have skilled hands," she praised the girl. "Tell your mother I am pleased and will require your services for another few days."

The maid curtsied and tried to hide her smile.

"Go on then," Runa encouraged her. "Get ready for the feast." Not a day over thirteen, it pleased Runa to see such a young, happy girl.

Captain Harald waited outside her chamber. When she opened the door, he looked her over carefully. "Be careful," he advised. "Dressed this way, you rival the beauty of the full moon."

They walked out of the women's quarters which were situated along the north wall of the temple. The great hall was located in a separate building not ten feet away from the sanctuary. Built to resemble a traditional longhouse, its high ceilings and length were overwhelming. Instead of a dirt floor covered in furs, beautiful colored stones had been carefully cut and fit together. Six hearths warmed the great space, the high table on the far side of the room.

"How many people are here tonight?" Runa asked.

"This hall can seat six hundred," he said.

"Six hundred?"

"Aye."

Fascinated, she looked about again, taking notice of the gold floor stands containing hundreds of candles. Overhead, in the uppermost rafters, hung Odin's banner—his messenger ravens, Huginn and Muninn, flying against a sea of red with scrolls in their beaks. The trestle tables were too numerous to count, silver goblets and matching platters graced each one. The scent of freshly baked bread and roasting meat made her stomach growl in appreciation.

"I am overwhelmed by the beauty and wealth of this place."

"Come." Harald ushered her to the back of the chamber where a short line had formed on the right side.

Guests were expected to greet the high priest and the other holy men. In the middle of the high table, close to the edge, sat a replica of Odin's crown, a raven skull decorated with oak branches. Two candles burned bright behind it, casting an eerie glow through the hollowed out eye sockets. Though Runa appreciated what it symbolized, it made her feel squeamish.

When their turn finally came, Captain Harald escorted her before the high priest who smiled down at her.

"Lady Runa. I trust your stay here has been comfortable."

She curtsied. "More than comfortable, sir."

"I am glad to hear it. Are you filled with joy tonight? Our lord Thor enjoys the smiles of pretty women."

"I am here to honor the great Thor and you."

Pleased with her answer, the high priest bowed his head. "I will set aside some time to speak with you in the next couple of days. Captain Harald, be sure to bring her to my solar."

"Aye." Harald bowed and shooed her away from the table.

"That's it?" she asked, surprised by the short audience with the high priest.

"There are hundreds of people to welcome, Lady Runa. Feel blessed though. On only three other occasions have I witnessed the high priest speak directly to a woman. The others were older and married."

"Does it mean anything important?" she pressed.

"It means you're too beautiful to resist."

Runa turned upon hearing Thorolf's deep voice and found him standing behind them. Dressed in black braies and a matching tunic embellished with gold thread, he looked more like a prince than a captain.

"Thank you for your service, Captain Harald," Thorolf said. "I can manage the lady from here. I believe your family awaits you."

"Aye." Harald smiled. "Until tomorrow, Lady Runa."

She watched him make his way down a long row of tables and disappear into the crowd.

"He's a good man."

"I agree."

"He deserves his own lands."

"You deserve a kiss," Thorolf squeezed her hand. "And a soft bed to roll around in."

Heat spread through her body. "And what has caused this sudden change in you, Sir?"

"Watching how the men reacted when you entered this hall. Not even the old ones could resist a peek, Runa. And I surely did more than that." His eyes were the color of a midnight sky, dark and seductive, ever focused on her face.

"If we weren't expected to stay for the feast, Captain Thorolf, I'd ask you to take me somewhere more quiet, even secluded, so I could get a better idea of what you mean."

"After the meat course," he said, "I will take you to such a place. All of your questions will be answered my sweet. Doubt will plague you no longer."

The threat attached to those seemingly innocent words made her weak in the knees. She sensed the urgency in him, saw it on his features. Thorolf wanted her. No more waiting. Tonight, she and the captain would be joined as one, so help her Odin.

Chapter Twenty-Five

Light and shadows.

Sun and moon.

Thunder and lightning.

Storms upon the sea and earth.

Great Thor, thunder born, son of Allfather.

Red giant, with a hammer of steel.

Power and immortality.

Youth and strength.

Truth and justice.

War and peace.

Love and fertility.

Great Thor.

God of war.

God of protection.

God of Thunder.

Hear us.

Walk among us.

Drink our mead.

Eat our meat.

Hear our song.

Great Thor.

Mighty son.

We honor you with blood.

Stay with us, great Thor.

Endure the ages.

Preserve our people.

Deliver us from our enemies.

Hear us, great Thor.

Thunder-born.

Protector of mankind.

Mighty Thor.

Hear us.

THE SONG ENDED and the high priest stood, saluting the crowd with his golden cup. "Long live Thor. Long live his faithful."

"Aye." The throng saluted, then drank.

Thorolf couldn't take his gaze off Runa. He'd never seen her look so beautiful before. Should he credit the candlelight? The gown she wore? The silver pins in her hair? The gold choker about her throat? *No*. Dressed in a sack she'd still shine. The glow in her cheeks when she looked up at him, her love unhidden from the world, made him crazy.

"Listen to me," he gripped her hand under the table. "We are failing miserably at keeping our feelings a secret."

"I cannot," she said. "This place has a way of making the truth come out."

Suspecting the potent wine had more to do with it, he poured her another serving. "Drink, Lady. Eat your fill. You'll need all your strength tonight."

She blushed and took a tiny sip.

"More bread, Sir?" a servant asked.

Thorolf froze when he heard that voice. A sound that triggered all the nightmares he'd banished to the deepest regions of his soul. Hatred welled up inside him. Bloodlust propelled him out of his chair as he grabbed the man's face, squeezing his cheeks so hard, Thorolf's fingers went numb. He dragged the whimpering bastard outside and across the clearing, with no regard for anything around him.

How many years had he waited to avenge his family? He stared heavenward, giving thanks to Thor. "On this night of all nights..."

His cousin's breathing was rapid and shallow. But Thorolf cared nothing about him, only that his blood must be spilled in order to appease the thunder god *and* himself. He lifted his murdering kinsman by the throat, his feet dangling.

"For my father, mother, and brother..." Eleven years ago, Thorolf's uncle, along with his three sons, lay siege to Thorolf's home in the middle of the night. "Feel their pain, hear their cries for mercy ring in your ears while I claim your worthless soul."

His cousin screamed as he slammed the man down on the ground. Thorolf ripped his long knife from his weapon belt and held it above his head.

"Thorolf, wait!"

At the sound of Runa's voice, he closed his eyes momentarily, trying to focus on what he needed to do instead of her. Though, if he could, he'd spare her the shock of watching this bloodshed.

More people gathered around now. It didn't matter. A life for a life. That's how Thorolf was raised. Blood for blood. His eyes popped open and then he stabbed his cousin in the heart over and over. *Father. Mother. Brother. People of Borg. All my suffering. Odin. Thor. Gift from the gods.* A hundred justifications for this violence existed. And, one-by-one, darted through his mind.

By the time someone gripped his shoulder from behind, urging him to drop the blade, Thorolf couldn't see straight. He studied his blood-soaked hand, two large gashes were on the underside where the knife had probably slipped.

"Come with me, Thorolf," the high priest said gently, holding on to his forearm as Thorolf stood. "We have much to discuss."

He nodded, ready to accept whatever punishment the high priest chose. It was forbidden to take a life on sacred ground unless offering a sacrifice to the gods or defending yourself.

Runa stepped in front of them, her eyes full of tears. "Thorolf," she whispered. "W-hat … who is that man?"

Instead of touching her, Thorolf caressed her with his eyes, taking in every beautiful inch of her being. If he faced death tonight, let Runa be the memory he carried with him to Hel. Captain Harald stood a few feet away and Thorolf waved him near. "Take care of her," he said, then let the priest lead him away.

Once seated inside the high priest's solar, the man served Thorolf a cup of ale, then sat down on the opposite side of the table. "I recognized you the first time we met, Captain Thorolf."

Void of emotion, Thorolf swallowed down the bitter drink. "Did you?"

"Aye. But I didn't press the issue because I sensed you didn't want to be identified. But now…" He looked about. "You've broken the law."

"A justified execution long overdue."

"Yes." The holy man leaned forward. "As the son of King Wyborn."

Hearing his father's name stung. He wrestled with the pain, wanting to choke the life out of the man for daring to speak it.

He took a deep breath. "How could you possibly know my face? I haven't been here in thirteen years."

"Some faces are unforgettable. And you, Prince Thorolf, have the same features as your good father."

"Do I?"

"And I pray the same sense of duty."

Thorolf wanted to chuckle at that fear-laced statement. But he didn't. Instead, he stretched his fingers on his right hand to alleviate some of the pressure building inside him. "Ask your questions, Priest. I will answer truthfully."

"Where have you been hiding?"

Thorolf's head snapped up in anger. "Rephrase your question."

"Where did you seek sanctuary after your family was killed?"

"Wherever I could. Away from the high north. Mostly in the Trondelag, working for shelter and training with weapons."

"How far you've come from the young boy who slit a goat's throat on Odin's altar all those years ago. Do you remember that Mabon holiday? King Wyborn brought you here to name you as his rightful heir and to be blessed by the gods."

"Aye."

"You were so eager to please him. I haven't seen a steadier hand on a boy since."

"The past is of no interest to me."

"It should be." The high priest stood. "Don't you want to know why your cousin was here posing as a servant?"

Did he have a choice? He nodded and pushed his empty cup toward the priest. "I thirst."

Obligingly, the priest refilled the vessel. "Three months ago, another bloody siege took place in Borg."

Thorolf shrugged. "A common thing."

"No," the priest disagreed. "Your father's loyal captains have waited for over a decade to find the right time to rebel against your uncle. If you only knew the intricate plan designed to slowly reap political discord among your people, how these great men planted the seeds of doubt in the minds of the commoners—in the ale houses and at the docks. Then you'd understand how desperate they were to restore your father's bloodline. To get you back. To crown you as king."

"My sire is dead. So is his kingdom."

"Nay, Prince Thorolf." The priest pounded his hand on the table. "Your kingdom thrives—ruled by a council until your return."

Unable to accept what the priest said while he stewed in the rage that had polluted his mind, Thorolf stood and headed for the door.

"Prince Thorolf, if not for your people's sake, what about for Lady Runa? Will you not claim your crown so you can marry the girl you love?"

Thorolf froze in his steps. "How do you know about the girl?"

"Sit back down, Thorolf, I have many things to explain still."

Chapter Twenty-Six

THE MAN LYING on the ground had died from multiple stab wounds. The snow surrounding him was no longer white but crimson. Stained with blood. Evidence of Thorolf's madness. Runa still couldn't believe how quickly he'd transformed from her happy lover to an enraged Berserker bent on violence.

"Have you no idea who he is?" she asked Captain Harald a second time.

"No, Lady. If I did, I'd say just to give you peace."

Curious onlookers continued to gather, whispering about Thorolf and pointing at Runa. She didn't like being the center of attention. Having already attracted the critical eyes of many guests in the great hall from her obvious affection for the captain, would these people think the dead stranger was Thorolf's rival? Her former love? Word would reach the Trondelag quickly and Roald would be that much more insistent on marrying her off to a man who lived in the farthest reaches of their country.

Two soldiers arrived with a sled and lifted the body onto it, then disappeared into the woods without a word to anyone.

"I'd like to follow those men, Captain."

He shook his head. "No. Whoever told them to retrieve the body wouldn't like it if we interfered."

"Then help me find Thorolf. I must know if he's safe."

"Judging by the way the high priest treated him, I'm sure he's in his solar now, not in a holding cell."

"Why would he kill him so mercilessly? He didn't give the man a chance to speak or defend himself. I've never seen anything like it. Thorolf dragged him out here by the throat, threw him down on the ground, and leapt on him like a ravenous beast." The scene played out in her mind over and over again. "Understand one thing about Thorolf, Captain, he's an honorable man. Disciplined and fair. Little unsettles him. And if it does, he has this way of controlling his emotions so no one else senses his anger. It's one of the reasons my brother appointed him to such a high position in his army."

"Are you familiar with his past?"

"Nay."

"Perhaps the stranger slighted him or hurt someone he cared for."

"No matter the reason, I wish I knew."

"Father," a young girl ran up to them, looking concerned.

"Mara." Harald greeted his daughter and kissed the top of her head. "Where are your mother and sister?"

"Waiting at home."

"Does your mother know you're out here?"

"No."

"How many times have I told you not to run off without permission?" Harald chastised the pretty, dark-haired girl.

"I needed to find you," Mara said. "I didn't like what our neighbors were saying about Lady Runa." She looked at Runa and smiled.

"I am pleased to meet you, Mara."

"As am I." She curtsied.

The captain had, indeed, told his family about her. The girl's genuine concern warmed Runa's heart. "I am sorry to keep your father away so long. If you return home and wait, I promise to bring you a gift tomorrow."

Mara's eyes went wide. "You swear it, Lady Runa?"

"I do."

Mara turned to the captain. "Is it all right for her to visit us?"

"Lady Runa is welcome anytime."

Mara clapped her hands and wrapped her arms around Harald's thighs, giving him a squeeze. "Thank you, Father. I will go home."

Runa watched the precious child sprint away.

"Mara is very sweet."

"And unruly." The captain scratched his head and grinned. "I'd have her no other way."

"You are a very fortunate man, Captain Harald."

"I don't know why, Lady Runa, but I've taken a great interest in your happiness and welfare since the day we met. Something about you reminds me of my daughters, which we've discussed before. For that very reason, I want you to know, sanctuary will always be given you under my humble roof."

Runa touched his arm. "I am ever grateful, Sir. Thank you."

"Which is why I must caution you now. This place is as volatile as a battleground. Holy men eliminating their rivals to scratch their way closer to the high priest. Kings and jarls from rival families seek counsel here. Sometimes they fight just beyond our lands. I will show you the burial mounds, how many fresh graves there are. Most of the maidens serving in Odin's sanctuary are forced here by their noble fathers, payment for past debts."

Runa narrowed her eyes, not wanting to believe it. "I don't understand."

"Thorolf told me about your ambition to become a temple

maiden. I beg you, put it out of your mind."

"Tis true," she admitted. "Though I'm not sure why Thorolf spoke with you about something so private. I can only assume he has a good reason." Like so many other things she'd recently discovered about him, she prayed he had an explanation. Especially for killing the stranger. "Take me to the sanctuary, Captain. I wish to wait for Thorolf there."

"Let me take you to your chamber or even to my cottage."

Runa shook her head. "I must insist."

Harald angled himself toward the temple. "Very well. Be prepared for a long night."

AFTER FINISHING A BOWL of stew with the high priest in his solar, Thorolf waited for the servants to clear the dishes and bring more mead so their enlightening conversation could continue. He'd been starved, as if he hadn't eaten in days. As for his thirst, he'd swallowed down six cups of mead already.

The door closed finally and the priest stationed himself next to Thorolf. "The respite is over, Prince Thorolf. We're alone and I can tell you why your cousin was here."

"Whatever you say won't change my mind. So why waste our time?"

"Are you drunk?"

"Drunk? Me?" Thorolf laughed hardily. "I've never been truly drunk. Though, as of late, I've been tempted to drink myself into a stupor just to forget who and what I am."

"Ah..." The priest smiled. "The most honest thing I've heard you say since joining me here."

Thorolf waved him off. "Most men would say the same. Life outside of this gilded cage is difficult at best."

"Not for you."

Thorolf stretched his long legs out and folded his hands behind his neck, sliding down in the padded chair. "A title won't change my fate. Or bring my family back."

"Maybe not. But if you'll just listen to reason, consider what I have to say."

"I can't stop you from talking."

"No." The holy man sighed, gazing skeptically at him. "But there's no guarantee you'll truly hear me."

"I've told you a dozen times already, any lingering connection I had to Borg is gone. It died the moment I ended my cousin's life."

"Your uncle plotted against his own brother, Prince Thorolf. Slaughtered your family in the middle of the night like a thief would. Tis no fault of your own. You were but a boy." The priest slapped the tabletop for emphasis, gaining Thorolf's full attention. "Your uncle let you escape."

Thorolf leaned forward. "What?"

"Yes. It wasn't accidental. Your uncle wanted you to live. To suffer. To wander the world as a broken man while he enjoyed the power and wealth that rightfully belonged to you."

"Why?"

"It is customary not to end the complete hereditary line of a kinsman, even if he's your enemy. The gods would surely punish the offender and the laws of men also forbid it."

"How beneficial," he said sarcastically, wiping his mouth with the back of his hand, feeling more and more uncivilized. Like he could kill anything that crossed his path, including a holy man in silk robes. "I am unfit for your company, Priest."

"Good," the priest said severely. "I want you mad. Determined to take back what's yours."

"I ask again, why?"

"If you don't claim the throne, there are others who will.

Men with less honor. Cousins of yours who share similar views as Jarl Skrymir. Bastards who would sooner divide this country than hold it together for the sake of our people."

"Fuck!" Thorolf shot up.

"You cannot deny the will of the gods."

"No," Thorolf spouted. "But I can resist them."

"Your father's captains spared the life of your cousin because your uncle let you live. Twas the right thing to do. Urd sought refuge here. I granted it so long as he agreed to live as a servant. To work for food and shelter. He lived in a sod-covered hut with only rags to wear."

Thorolf shrugged off his rage long enough to listen closely.

"I prefer the comfort of my *gilded cage*, Prince Thorolf. To a man such as you, I might appear weak. But I've earned my position of power. As you've earned your title as a captain in Jarl Roald's army. I am endowed by the gods to punish and pardon men who commit heinous crimes. Mercy is at my disposal. For commoners and kings alike."

This is what Thorolf had waited for. The high priest was about to pass judgement on him. "Get it over with."

"For murdering your cousin, Urd, I command you to wed Lady Runa, sister of Jarl Roald, six days hence at sundown, and then reclaim your throne in Borg. You will unite two powerful families through this marriage. In so doing, I will gain an ally in the north. Your uncle neglected his duty to this holy place. I need gold and more men."

The finality of what the priest said made his whole body shake. Marry Runa? Do to her what she despised her brother for? Force her into a union she didn't want? And become a king? "If I refuse?"

"My decision is nonnegotiable, Prince Thorolf. I've already sent for an envoy from Borg. They will arrive in a few days. I will have the honor of crowning you king at the same time I preform your wedding ceremony. My order will be posted for the public to see. I suggest taking some time to consider your good fortune. And if at all possible, inform your beautiful bride that she's going to be a queen." The priest moved to his chair and ignored Thorolf.

Thorolf crossed the room then, ready to hide from the reality of his new world. The priest had already sent for representatives from his home, *before* Thorolf killed Urd. Stopping at the door, he leaned his forehead against the wood, contemplating his future. Considering the joy of taking Runa to wife and returning to his beautiful home. Of thanking the loyal men who avenged his family. Good fortune had, indeed, smiled down on him today, whether he liked it or not.

Suddenly, he wanted every man alive to know his true identity, to know Lady Runa belonged to him.

"I will do as you command," he informed the priest before opening the door and stepping out, no longer a captain, but a prince.

SEEING THOROLF SAFE thrilled Runa. She jumped up as soon as he exited the high priest's solar. Although he looked exhausted and perhaps a bit irritated, he was back. "Thorolf." She rushed to his side.

"What are you doing here?" He took her hands, holding them tight. Then he eyed Captain Harald. "How long have you been waiting?"

"Since they collected the man's body from outside," Harald answered, still sitting on the bench across the passageway.

"Tell me," Runa said, anxious and hopeful that the high priest had been fair. "Will there be a punishment? Is it severe?"

Thorold stroked her fingers reassuringly. "Many things have changed, Runa. I was going to wait until tomorrow, but since you are here…" He looked in the direction of the sanctuary, to Odin's altar. "Come with me."

He dragged her to the center of the vast chamber, staring up at the ceiling, smiling at the imagery of Allfather. "The gods have intervened on my behalf, Runa. *Our* behalf," he corrected himself, staring at her. "I've prayed night and day, begged Odin to reveal a way we could be together as man and wife."

Impossible so long as Roald insisted she marry a jarl or prince. But she didn't want to ruin the moment. "Tell me."

"I don't know where to start," he said, leading her up the steps to the dais where the holy men usually stood. "I've not been completely honest with you or Jarl Roald. I am not who you think I am."

Hope bloomed in her heart. Perhaps the high priest had appointed him to a position of authority with the temple guard. They could live here, free from her brother. "Title, wealth, power, none of it matters to me, Thorolf. I accept you for who you are—the man I've always loved. My heart cries out for you."

Passion darkened his eyes then and he tugged her closer. "Those words mean more to me than anything, sweet Runa. I believe you, for you've proven your love and dedication over and over again. You offered me your body and heart without the promise of marriage. Willing to risk your future on our happiness."

"I'd do it again."

"Aye."

"Now tell me. Why are we at the altar?"

"You know only bits and pieces about my past."

"Yes, you're from Borg, a kingdom far north. The great

peninsula where giants are rumored to live." She smiled. "Men like you."

"I've forgotten the legends of my birthplace." He chuckled. "It is true; the fiercest warriors come from Borg. Do you know who King Wyborn was?"

"The murdered ruler? The king with the greatest fleet in Norway?"

"Aye, the very man."

"News of his demise reached our home long ago. I was but a child. I remember my father sacrificing a bull on his behalf, seeking the protection of the gods. Did you know the king? Did the man you killed have a hand in his death?"

"He was my cousin. King Wyborn was his uncle."

"U-uncle?" She let go of his hands. "I don't understand."

"I am not without a home, Runa." He dropped to one knee in front of her. "I am King Wyborn's son. The only surviving member of the royal family." He confessed everything.

Runa blinked several times, wondering if this was a dream. Why hadn't he trusted her enough to confide in her? Especially after everything that had happened. They were lovers. Friends. Connected in a way most men and women never experienced. "You should have told me sooner."

"I couldn't."

"Why now?"

"The high priest recognized me days ago, when I showed up asking for help. He said nothing, waiting for the right time to confront me. But now..."

"Your cousin is dead, he had no choice," she finished his thought.

"Aye."

"And you are eager to return home."

"I am desperate to keep you. I'd stay a humble captain of the guard if it pleased you. If I could still have you. Marry you. Live in peace in the Trondelag."

She caressed his cheek. "Are you offering to make me a queen, Thorolf?"

He gazed up at her, his beautiful eyes as turbulent as a stormy ocean. "I'm offering you the world, Runa. Me. My people. The kingdom of Borg. My army. My broken heart. Marry me, here, in the presence of the gods."

Tears streamed down her cheeks. How could it be? All this time, Captain Thorolf had really been Prince Thorolf. No, King Thorolf. And he'd catered to her every need without complaint. Protected her. Followed her about like a servant. Believed in her because he loved her. "Aye," she said. "I'll have you, as captain *or* king."

He roared with joy and lifted her high above his shoulders, spinning her about in his arms. "I am happiest man alive, Runa. No one can keep us apart now. The high priest has sanctioned our marriage. Not even the gods can overrule what he commands."

She didn't care about the details. Runa just wanted to be alone with Thorolf, free to love him. "We have plans to make, milord."

Thorolf gripped her hand. "And many lessons to learn, don't we, my perfect queen?"

Heat spiraled through her body as she imagined his big warm hands touching her everywhere. "I love you, Thorolf."

"I love you, Runa. Let us celebrate with a glass of wine." He led her away from the temple and back to the great hall, where people were still celebrating Thurseblot.

Chapter Twenty-Seven

"SURRENDERING TO THE high priest is an act of lunacy, Jarl Olvir. Why waste time in the high north when we can turn these horses around and be back in the Trondelag within three days?"

Olvir slowed his mount, facing his loyal captain. "You consider me an honest man, Rolf?"

"Aye."

"And you are fully aware of my conversion to Christianity while serving under Prince Ivarr in Northumbria?"

"Your father made sure to let everyone in his household know about it. However, it changes nothing. Your sire's men will follow you."

"You misunderstood me. As a Christian, I must confess my sins and submit myself to the authorities for the crime I committed. Since there isn't a church within hundreds of miles, I must settle for the next best thing. The high priest will hear of my situation, *from me*."

"Why not wrap the rope around your own neck now?" Rolf sounded angry, but looked worried.

Olvir appreciated his concern, but he must stay true to his faith. "I am not afraid to die," he revealed. "In fact, I welcomed death until a couple days ago. My father's abuse left me with no choice but to pray to my God for a quick end. Another sin.

Absolution is attainable, but only if I publicly admit to my wrongdoing."

"There is no mercy for Christians this far north. They'd sooner flay you and sacrifice you to Odin, then risk letting you spread the word of the White Christ like a plague. Turn back, milord, spare yourself. Find another way to make amends. I have heard stories about self-flagellation, how monks flog themselves as a form of religious discipline."

Impressed that Rolf knew so much about his faith, he smiled kindly. "Aye, it is true. Though no one is supposed to know when a monk does so, some seek attention and praise from their superiors for suffering through the daily practice. I am not a man of the cloth. This form of purification isn't available to a scribe or nobleman. I would have to join an order, pledge eternal service to Christ, and give away all of my holdings or pick an heir to endow with my father's title."

"I know another way."

As they emerged from the woods, Olvir stopped and dismounted, wanting a drink of water and some bread. "Tell me."

Rolf joined him. "Convert."

"Again?"

"Aye.

Abandon Christ to save his own life? *A coward's way out*, he heard his father accuse. One thing Olvir had never considered himself was a coward. Only his sire thought so. Ivarr had praised him endlessly for his service across the North Sea. Even after he pledged faith in the Saxon God. But the Danes had been living among the Saxons for years and were more accepting of their customs. A wise conqueror allowed his thralls to worship whatever gods they chose so long as they worked and paid tribute. It kept the peace.

"I'd rather face cold, hard death than lie. Let the high priest deal with me as fairly or cruelly as he wishes."

"Olvir the Honest will be known throughout the northlands before this is all over," Rolf said, swallowing a swig of warm wine from a skin Olvir offered him.

"We are only a few miles from the temple. When we arrive, find accommodations for yourself. You must tell no one of your affiliation with me until I find out what my punishment will be."

"As you command, milord."

They split a loaf of bread in a hurry, then mounted, riding full speed.

As the fires in the courtyard outside the temple became visible from the hilltop they'd climbed, that's when Olvir realized he was being followed by someone other than Rolf. He'd spent a fair amount of time in this holy place, knowing the routine of the guards. Bonfires were lit every night not only to keep warm by but also to honor the gods. Those flames represented the eternal fire burning in Odin's heart and hearth in Asgard. Soldiers made routine checks around the perimeter of the complex, always prepared to fight.

Olvir turned his horse about, hoping to locate Captain Rolf. But in the darkness, it was hard to see far away. "Rolf?" he called. But no one answered.

"Did you get lost my friend?"

Someone reached up and yanked Olvir from the saddle. "What are you doing here?"

Olvir stumbled and fell to his knees. "Who are you?" Then he recognized the bearded giant towering above him, *Captain Thorolf.*

THOROLF GLARED DOWN at the half-man he'd banished from Jarl Roald's home a short time ago. Filthy traitor—a believer in the

White Christ and a man in love with Runa. "State your purpose here or I will squash you with my heel like the insignificant creature you are."

Olvir staggered to his feet, brushing the snow from his backside. "Captain Thorolf. Have you sold your services to the temple now?"

Is that what this weakling thought of him? A simple man-at-arms? "I will ask the questions."

"Very well. I am here to seek an audience with the high priest."

"Unbelievers are forbidden here."

Olvir huffed out a frustrated breath. "I will take my chances with the priest."

"Only if I let you pass."

"Where is my guard, Rolf?"

"Stopped by my men a few yards south. I've been tracking you for over an hour, Olvir. And if I were any other man, you'd be dead. Speak frankly before I lose patience."

"My father is dead. I've come to seek counsel."

Thorolf knew the pain of losing a parent. The sad news changed his mind about how to deal with Olvir. "I am sorry for your loss."

"Don't be," Olvir said. "I killed him."

Unprepared for his words, Thorolf gave him a sideways look. "Did I misunderstand you?"

"No. I shot an arrow through my father's eye in front of his captains and guests. I am surprised word hasn't reached here already. I've come to face the council for my crime."

The thought of a son slaying his own sire brought back many painful memories. Thorolf grabbed a fistful of Olvir's tunic and gave him a shake. "Why have you done this?"

Limp in his grasp, Olvir remained silent.

Thorolf shoved him away, disgusted by his calm demeanor. "I will escort you to the high priest then. Don't expect mercy. There's been too much bloodshed in these parts lately. The high priest has had his fill of violence. As have I." He searched Olvir's face for any signs of regret, finding none.

"It's truth you seek? I understand completely, Captain. Why would a man kill his own father? Jarl Otkel was cruel. He beat my mother and me. Thankfully, she died a long time ago, escaping his hatred. Unfortunately, I didn't."

There were other ways to deal with his father. Banishment. Challenging him for control of the jarldom. Not murder. "Save your words for the priest. You wouldn't like my ruling."

Olvir frowned. "Captain Thorolf, for now, I am a jarl. I expect you to show me the courtesy and respect due my title."

Thorolf made a show of looking surprised. "Things have changed drastically for me as well, Jarl Olvir. I, too, have gained a title. You will address me as Prince Thorolf. Now get on your horse. Until the high priest says otherwise, I am holding you as a prisoner. Murderers cannot be permitted to roam free in the northlands."

Olvir did as he commanded, climbing into the saddle and surrendering the reins. Thorolf rode in the direction of the temple, disappointed he hadn't found a trace of Jarl Skrymir on his typical evening rounds, but pleased he'd captured a romantic rival of his future wife.

Chapter Twenty-Eight

THOROLF ROSE FROM his chair out of respect for the high priest and the judges, as did all the spectators in the council chamber. Olvir and his errant captain were in chains, surrounded by four temple guards, at the center of the room. The hearing could not be delayed with Thorolf's wedding only two days out.

Once the high priest took a seat, a man in black robes pounded the end of his walking staff on the stone floor to gain the attention of the crowd. "We are gathered to hear testimony against Olvir and Captain Rolf, rebels and murderers of the honorable Jarl Otkel from the Trondelag. Let all men present serve as witnesses to what is shared. And may the gods provide guidance and clarity to the judges, that the accused are dealt with fairly and swiftly, so help me Odin."

"So help us Odin," the throng repeated, then sat back down.

"Olvir, stand and be recognized," the high priest said.

He did.

"I heard your testimony in my chamber a couple nights ago when you were arrested by Prince Thorolf on your way to the temple."

"Aye."

"Do you still stand by what you said?"

"I do."

"And you are prepared to accept whatever this council rules, even if it means forfeiting your life?"

"I will tell you what I have shared with other men. I am not afraid to die. This world is a better place without my father in it. He was an arrogant and dangerous man. Prone to fits of rage and drunkenness."

"You have described better than half the men in Scandinavia," one of the judges commented.

The crowd laughed.

"I care little for what happens in other homes, Sir," Olvir stated, looking at the judge. "Each man is responsible for his own steading and family. I can only tell you what happened to me and my beloved mother. Her back was as scarred as mine. My sire was free with the whip and fist. Ask any of his captains, including Rolf, who has committed no crime. I beg you to free him from these chains." Olvir held up his hands, the irons clinking together as he shifted. "I killed my father without premeditation. No one knew what I was doing. And Captain Rolf is the most celebrated soldier in my father's personal guard."

"Why did he travel with you?" the high priest asked.

"To convince me to return home."

The priest turned to Rolf. "Does this not make you guilty? Why would you try to protect the man that cut down your master?"

Rolf cleared his throat and stood. "Can a Christian find true justice in this court? You'll judge him for his faith, not his alleged crime."

"Alleged?" another council member asked. "The man has confessed. There's innocent blood on his hands. That is irrefutable."

"Is it?" Rolf shook his head. "See for yourself then. Direct one of these guards to remove Olvir's tunic."

The judges whispered amongst themselves, the one closest to the high priest leaned close to him.

"Very well, Captain," the priest said. "Donvar, cut this man's sark open."

The guard nodded, then spun Olvir around, using a long knife to bear his back. As soon as the scars were visible, the judges gasped in shock. Even Thorolf couldn't resist looking. He moved closer, eyeing the ugly, raised scars with disgust. It reminded him of a map, all the deep lines crisscrossing over his spine, from the base of his neck to Olvir's hips. The man hadn't exaggerated. The pain he must have suffered as a boy made Thorolf grit his teeth. What humiliation and shame he must have felt facing his maniacal father every day. No wonder he accepted a post in Northumbria under the guise of training as a soldier. Twas his only escape.

"The council is satisfied, Olvir. You may sit," the high priest directed him, his tone softer.

"Now that you've seen the evidence first-hand, milord, spare Olvir's life. He's suffered enough."

The high priest raised his hand. "Captain Rolf, your plea doesn't fall on deaf ears. I understand your way of thinking more than you know. Donvar, free the captain."

It pleased Thorolf to see the truth respected in this place. He gazed about the lofty room, at the high ceilings and stone walls. A guilty man would be easily intimidated. A statue of Tyr, the god of law and justice, stood at the forefront of the chamber, very near the council's high table. Black banners with single runic symbols stitched on them decorated the walls. Thorolf could decipher most of them, justice, truth, honor, wisdom, bravery, servitude... However, there were a few he didn't recognize.

"What is your earliest memory of your father hitting you, Olvir?" the high priest queried.

"Sometimes my memory fails me, sir," Olvir admitted. "The days and weeks have blended together. But I believe I was a boy of four seasons, sitting at the feast table with my father. Instead of eating, I threw a skin ball one of the captains had given me across the room. It landed in a dignitary's bowl of stew. My sire snatched me up and slapped my face repeatedly. Even our honored guest begged for leniency, but my father refused. He beat me unconscious and tossed me on the floor."

The high priest's face twisted in disbelief.

"He speaks honestly," Rolf said. "I was there."

The spectators couldn't remain silent any longer—Olvir was slowly winning their support.

"And your mother?" the priest asked. "Did she try to protect you? How did your father deal with her?"

"He never bruised her face," Olvir pointed out. "She was very pretty and my father relied on her gentle nature to sooth the fiercest of men when treaties or other business brought visitors to our steading. But her back and thighs were marred and bloody more times than I can count. Our female thralls often whispered about it, wept for her, complained about how rough my father was with her in the bedchamber."

"He raped her?" a council member asked.

"Aye. Many times."

Again, the council members whispered to each other.

"Why didn't you stay in Northumbria? Prince Ivarr asked you to. Didn't you find purpose there? Peace?" the high priest pressed.

"My father expected me to return. Like a fool, I hoped to please him with my accomplishments, to finally give him a reason to be proud of his only son."

"There is no reason to hear more," a spectator called out. "Free this man."

"Any father who beats an innocent babe deserves to die," another said.

"Free Olvir." One-by-one, men stood and raised their fists in protest of the council continuing with the hearing.

The man in the black robes beat the floor with his staff again. "Silence, or the guards will clear the chamber."

"Prince Thorolf," the high priest said. "You encountered Olvir on the road to the temple. I would hear your opinion in this matter."

Thorolf noted the faces of the six judges at the high table. Everyone was expected to remain impartial when sitting in judgement of another man. But Thorolf knew how hard that could be. Especially when ruling on a case involving a mortal enemy to the old gods—a Christian convert born in Norway.

"I will give it." Thorolf approached the high table. "Olvir spared no detail. He came here of his own free will, acknowledging the risk he took subjecting himself to a council of men who worship Allfather. At first, I too hated the man for slaughtering his sire. My own story kept me from seeing the evidence before me. Nothing could justify him murdering his father. Nothing. But after hearing his testimony again and affirming the disfiguring scars on his body, I am certain mercy is called for in this case." He drifted toward Olvir. "You loved your father?"

"Aye."

"How do you feel now? Would you reconsider what you did if given a chance?"

"I'd give my right eye for a second chance with him."

"Where would you go if this council sets you free, Olvir?"

"Back to the Trondelag to repair what damage has been done."

"And if your father's men are unwilling to serve you, to forgive, what will you do?"

"I will choose an heir from among my kinsmen, appoint him as the new jarl, and then leave Norway behind forever."

"What if one of your sire's captains kills you?"

Olvir's shoulders sagged. "I'd ask this council to take no action against him. Even if I am exonerated, I must live with my sin forever."

"Sin?" the high priest said. "Our gods endowed this council with the right to judge you. If found innocent, Olvir, there is no emotional burden to carry."

"By the laws of this land, perhaps. But a different law governs my heart." He raised his head. "It is a hard thing to explain to a man who doesn't share my faith. My guilt is the first step toward gaining forgiveness from my God."

"That is for you to decide," the high priest said. "Before we stepped into this chamber, I directed the council members to set aside any prejudice against your religion. Because you came here without being summoned, for braving the ridicule you might be subjected to on ground consecrated to Odin, because your back has been scarred by your father's rage, and your heart forever broken by the loss of your mother, I find no fault in you, Jarl Olvir of the Trondelag. But, I alone cannot choose." The high priest stood. "And I shall not remain here, for if these men condemn you, I will overturn their ruling."

The high priest exited the chamber, followed by several priests who attended him.

The room fell silent for several long moments. Thorolf wondered who would speak first. He gazed at the council, then at Olvir, a man he'd severely misjudged. Olvir possessed a face like an open scroll. All his emotions showed in his eyes. Something Thorolf had worked diligently to overcome. The more a man could read in your eyes, the more dangerous it was. But for Olvir, under these circumstances, it was likely the one thing that would save him.

"The facts surrounding this case are highly unusual," one of the judges said. "And in no way, if we decide in your favor, Olvir, should it encourage other sons to murder their sires."

"Aye," Olvir agreed.

The members withdrew from the chamber then, calling for a brief reprieve.

"I cannot thank you enough for speaking on my behalf, Prince Thorolf," Olvir addressed him.

"Do not think I've forgotten your actions from the night at Jarl Roald's feast. You are a Christian, still my enemy. But truth must always prevail. And no child should ever face the violence and devastation you did."

Olvir's eyes were wet with tears. This time, Thorolf saw the pain and regret in them he'd sought out before. "I will remember your fairness, whether we are friends or enemies."

"A day will come when you challenge the old ways, Olvir. That much has been foreseen by the oracles and spaewives who give counsel to Norway's kings and chieftains. On that day, I will seek you out first, my sword against yours. My life or yours, so help me Odin."

Olvir swallowed hard, then spoke. "Until that time, Prince Thorolf, I will consider you an ally."

Just as Thorolf intended to reply, the council members returned. Thorolf gave Olvir a last look, then returned to his seat across the room.

"Olvir, son of Otkel, we find you not guilty of the crime of murder. You will be set free and must leave this holy place, along with your captain, never to return, unless you choose to offer yourself to Odin again."

After the judge had spoken, Olvir dropped to his knees and bowed his head. Thorolf knew he was praying to the White Christ, the enemy God he loathed. A guard lifted Olvir to his feet and removed his wrist and ankle irons.

"Go, Jarl Olvir," the judge said.

Rolf followed his jarl out of the room, his hand never leaving the hilt of his sword.

Chapter Twenty-Nine

"WHY I AM expected to stay indoors until the eve of my wedding," Runa complained to her hostesses. She'd been temporarily moved to the house where the temple maidens lived. "I am unaccustomed to this isolation."

"Try to accept it," Haldana, the eldest of the maidens, urged. "You are to be crowned a queen. The high priest cannot risk your life while under his care. Escorts will take you to the great hall each night for the eventide meal. Do we lack any of the comforts you are used to?"

Runa looked about the expansive solar where the women lounged. There were comfortable couches and padded chairs, tables filled with bright cloth to sew, boxes of jewelry and hair adornments, combs and pins, gowns to wear, and even a collection of scrolls with stories honoring the gods. In the far corner, two tubs were available to soak in, an assortment of oils and perfumed soaps to enjoy.

The dream of becoming a temple maiden had been swiftly ended the moment she entered this comfortable prison. The women here were coddled and protected, spoiled with every luxury, but their freedom forever gone. Like prized pets, they lived according to the high priest's will. Surrounded by armed guards on the outside, put on display during feasts and holidays, hidden away the rest of the time.

"Would it help if I showed you what the high priest has selected as your wedding gown?" Haldana asked.

"It is here already?"

"Aye. Sent over yesterday."

"Why does he keep a collection of women's garments in his storerooms?"

The maids chuckled.

"Our benefactors pay tribute to the temple in many ways. Silk and other rare treasures are perfectly acceptable. I am sure you will find it exquisite, Lady Runa."

Haldana snapped her fingers and two younger girls scurried from the chamber. "There are other gifts to enjoy, too."

Knowing there was nothing she could do to escape the confines of the house, Runa sat down on one of the couches, hoping she'd see Thorolf today—before the nighttime meal. Everything he'd shared with her still weighed heavy on her conscience. They weren't given much time alone. Every precaution had to be taken to ensure that their wedding was conducted under the strictest of traditions.

The high priest would give no one a chance to challenge the legitimacy of her and Thorolf's union. Especially her brother.

Minutes later, the girls returned with two crates. Runa pretended she could picture herself dressed as a happy bride, surrounded by loving family members and friends. She envisioned her mother, father, and brothers, all smiles and good wishes. But it would never be. With her parents dead and Roald sure to punish her for breaking his trust, she knew she'd never be welcomed in the Trondelag again.

Then there was Thorolf. What would her brother do to him? It didn't matter her future husband out-ranked him or possessed more power. He'd broken a sacred oath to her family, regardless of the fact he'd sworn allegiance to her before they left for Prince Axel's home.

"Do you like it, milady?" One of the girls interrupted her thoughts.

Runa looked up and immediately admired the spring green gown the girl was holding. Made of silk and embroidered with silver and gold thread, the bodice was covered in delicate blossoms resembling little bells. The second girl showed her a pair of matching slippers and Runa smiled and nodded with approval.

"These come from Northumbria," Haldana said. "Part of a significant estate that was plundered and claimed by one of the chieftains north of here. The other box contains a veil and silver chains meant to go about your waist. Come, do try it on now. If we need to make any alterations, they must be started tonight."

Wanting to be kind, Runa did as she asked, allowing the maids to stand her up and strip her clothes off. The soft material of the new gown settled over her head and shoulders like air, the length falling to her feet.

"Now the shoes," one of the girls said, kneeling in front of her and sliding the first slipper on her left foot.

"How do you feel?" Haldana asked, stepping back and eyeing her head-to-toe.

Runa gazed down at herself, running her palms down the skirt. "I've never worn something so fine."

"Few have," Haldana said. "There is more, chosen for you by Prince Thorolf."

When had her betrothed found time to select a new wardrobe for her? It made her feel warm all over, that he'd take such special care of her. "If only I could see myself."

"You shall." Haldana took her hand and directed her to a sub-chamber.

Runa had never seen a higher quality looking glass before.

Rectangular in shape and hanging on the wall, she could take in half her body. If she stepped back several feet, nearly her full form became visible in the pounded metal.

"This gown is a perfect fit, made for you, Lady Runa."

Admittedly, Haldana was right. Runa admired her reflection, liking how the light-green silk complimented her dark hair and the green of her eyes. "Thank you," she said, appreciative of how well she was being treated. "Is there time to see the other gowns? To try them on?"

Haldana gave her a big smile. "Nothing soothes a woman's woes as well as a pretty gown."

"I am sorry for being so difficult, Haldana. If I appear ungrateful…"

"Please." The woman squeezed her hand. "Before we were pledged to Odin, we were the daughters of men, too. Kings, princes, jarls, and wealthy merchants. Our sires gave us away like livestock to pay debts or to be rid of us because they remarried and their new wives didn't want any reminders of their husbands' past lives. Some of us mourn the loss of our families, our freedom. Others celebrate what we have discovered here—a new family—sisters forever."

"If you only knew…"

"How desperately you wanted to serve Odin? To become one of us?"

"How did you know?"

"When you visited us the other day, I recognized the look in your eyes, though you tried to hide it. I came here ten years ago. My father and mother wanted to keep me, but I refused to listen and begged day and night. After a year, they gave me their blessing. My brother escorted me here. I haven't seen my family since."

"In ten years?" It pained Runa to think about never seeing

Konal and Silvia, Haakon, and Eva, her beloved sister-in-law, again. What about the children? She adored her nephews and niece. Runa studied her new friend's pain-filled expression. "I'm a fool. Naïve. How silly I must look to a woman like you."

"Never. Odin has blessed me, Runa. My family has prospered. Though I am not highborn, my father has earned enough gold to secure a noble woman for my eldest brother to marry. Their children will be titled. My brother called lord." Haldana stepped closer and whispered. "Though I am forbidden to marry, I have found companionship here."

"With a priest?" she asked dumbly.

Haldana's pretty brows knitted together. "Dear Odin, no. The priests don't know what to do with their pikks beyond taking a piss," she laughed. "My lover is a commander in the temple guard. In charge of the men who defend our house."

Runa enjoyed the way Haldana's eyes lit up when she talked about her man. She desperately hoped her love for Thorolf showed on her face. "Are you in love?"

"Aye," she admitted. "Nothing can dissuade me from being with him."

"Not even…" Runa stopped herself from saying *death*.

"The threat of being sacrificed?"

"Aye," Runa said, ashamed for even thinking it.

"My father paid a fortune to keep me from being part of the annual lottery. But half of the girls in this house are not as fortunate. The gods must be compensated for their continued blessings."

"So it is true?"

"A virgin's blood is the purest."

Runa cared for this woman—knew she deserved a better life. "Tis unfortunate men aren't offered to the gods as often."

"They are too valuable to sacrifice. Only every nine years at the Thing. But those men volunteer, guaranteed a seat at Odin's feast table in Valhalla."

Runa embraced her new friend, hoping there was a way she could help her. "I'm ready to see the gowns my betrothed picked for me."

"Very well. If you'll wait here, I'll get them."

Runa waited until she was alone to thank the gods for keeping her from making a fatal mistake. Perhaps Odin had nothing to do with it. Maybe her mother, or even her sire who hadn't showed her much love when he was alive, had interceded on her behalf and given her a better future than she would have chosen for herself. Whatever the reason, she would always remember her good fortune and strive to keep any girl from choosing a life as a temple maiden.

Chapter Thirty

SEATED IN A private solar designated for visiting nobles, Thorolf awaited the arrival of the captains the high priest had summoned from Borg. Harald stood at his side, the obvious choice as his new personal adviser. Thorolf would offer to take his family north and provide him with a home and plot of land, as Runa had wanted. There were so many decisions to make, people to meet, trust to be won.

The door opened and Thorolf stood.

The high priest, followed by his attendants and five men dressed in traditional Borg regalia entered the room. Years couldn't erase Thorolf's memories of home. His father's men wore black leather tunics with red stitching forming the cloudberry blossoms that dominated the landscape in Borg.

"Prince Thorolf," the high priest spoke. "Your captains have just arrived. I offered them food and drink, but they refused and insisted on seeing you immediately."

Thorolf nodded. Why put off the inevitable? Either these brave men would welcome him as their lord or they'd reject him. His gaze wandered to one of the five, an exceptionally tall man with a copper-colored beard and icy eyes. There was no mistaking the identity of the older man. "Dreng?" He stepped forward. "Is it you?"

The warrior cocked his head, taking in Thorolf. "Depends

who asks, Boy."

"Thorolf." His old teacher hadn't changed much, a streak of gray in his long curls and deeper lines around his serious eyes. "I have waited for this moment."

Dreng dropped to his knee. "Prince Thorolf. We have waited over a decade to be reunited."

The other soldiers did the same. "Prince Thorolf," they chorused, pounding their fists against their chests, then kneeling before him.

As his father would have done, Thorolf stood before the first and rested his hand on his head. "Etzel, Odin bless you for your show of loyalty."

Etzel gazed up at him. "My sword is yours, King Thorolf."

Thorolf moved on to the next man. "I remember you well, Igor. May the gods give you glory in battle for coming here today."

Thorolf ended with Captain Dreng. "Stand before me as an equal. My sire favored you above all others and I will have it no other way."

The big man rose and embraced Thorolf. "You have grown into a man."

Thorolf slapped his back affectionately and then pulled back so he could see his mentor clearly. "Not half the beast you are."

Dreng patted his stomach. "Tis the fault of the cooks. I'm as wide as I am tall."

"My homeland thrives?"

"We're twice as strong as we were ten years ago," the captain said. "However, the throne sits empty."

Everyone stood then and chose a seat.

"The high priest has told me many things, Dreng. And though I was reluctant, at first, to claim my father's throne, nothing can deter me now. I will honor my family and people."

"Your uncle slaughtered sixty women and children the night you escaped. We lost thirty soldiers in the fight. The shrewd bastard hired a hundred mercenaries to usurp power from your father. Murdered your family, then dug a hole in the ground and buried them indiscriminately in unmarked graves."

The harrowing news settled on Thorolf like a black shroud. "And where are my parents' bodies now? My brother?"

"In the ground still, waiting for their son and brother to come home and honor them properly."

Thorolf shrugged off the pain. There'd be time to mourn them later, once he stood before their burial mound. "Why did you rise up against my uncle now? What changed?"

Dreng looked at the other captains and sucked in a breath. "Your uncle stole our firstborn babes and threatened to kill them if we didn't pledge allegiance to him. Once the people learned of the deaths of your family and tasted your uncle's brutality, fear crippled them. Life slowly returned to normal. But we never forgot you."

Two braziers provided warmth in the room. Thorolf stared into the flames, wondering if he should accept the captain's explanation without further question. He had no right to judge these loyal men too harshly. "Where are your children now?"

"Safe and growing," Dreng answered. "We all have sons and daughters. My eldest carries your father's name. And Vestar's youngest boy is named Thorolf."

"How did my uncle die?"

"The same way your father did. Cut like a wild pig and hung by his feet in the courtyard for all to see."

"My aunt?"

Dreng stared at the floor and grew silent.

"Captain? How did my aunt die?"

"We gave her to the mercenaries your uncle hired as a

prize," Vestar said.

The harsh reality of what they'd done to avenge his family would never leave him. "And those men?"

"Executed," Dreng spoke again.

"My uncle had *four* children."

"The two eldest boys were hanged. The daughter, Ellisif, was sold at a slave market in Baghdad. As for the youngest boy…"

"You know of his fate?" Thorolf queried.

"The high priest informed us." Dreng shifted in his chair. "No mercy was shown to you. To King Wyborn or our queen."

"The girl must be rescued from her bondage. She was but a babe when my uncle betrayed my family. I will not have her blood on my hands."

"Aye," Dreng said. "What do you want me to do with her?"

"Bring her home, Dreng. Treat her with decency and remind her that mercy will always be given to the truly innocent. I will accept her as a sister. And when its time, she will wed a good man."

"If I have displeased you in any way…"

Thorolf held up his hand. "The time for violence is over. Let us all forgive our pasts and start anew. I am not here to judge you. Only to try and understand what I have to return to. I am a stranger. Until a few days ago, a sell-sword with no home."

"You are no stranger," Etzel disagreed. "But a lost son. We can no longer accept our lives continuing on the savage course they've taken since your father's death. Though we prosper, a council is no substitute for a true king."

Thorolf nodded. "The rest of you share these feelings? The people want me to return? You are prepared to bend a knee to me as the rightful heir and king? To entrust me with your lives?"

The high priest walked over to Dreng. "Captain, did you

bring the crown?"

"Aye." Dreng reached into the leather bag draped over his shoulder and produced something wrapped in skins. "Here."

The priest opened the bundle and smiled at what he saw. "The symbol of your sovereignty, Prince Thorolf. Will you have it?"

Thorolf eyed the circlet of gold and silver. It had graced the heads of his kinsmen for twenty generations. He hesitated to answer for a brief moment, remembering what his old life had been like. Simple. A soldier who served Jarl Roald. "I will." He stood, shoulders squared, proud to be the son of King Wyborn and Queen Toril. "I pledge a reign of peace and prosperity if the gods will allow it. If any try to harm us, I will destroy them. This I swear on my own life."

"Good," the high priest said, then gestured at one of his attendants.

The servant placed a red pillow on the floor in front of Thorolf.

"Kneel, Prince Thorolf," the high priest directed.

Thorolf didn't understand. He thought he was to be crowned tomorrow evening at his wedding.

"There is no reason to wait," the holy man said as if he'd heard Thorolf's thought.

As Thorolf knelt, his captains surrounded him, including Harald.

The high priest held the circlet over Thorolf's head. "Let every man be subject to your power. The gods ordain you. The people choose you. By divine right, your sword will defend against evil. Your name will prevail. Your sons will follow in your footsteps, great conquerors for Allfather, soldiers for justice. None in the nine realms have the authority to challenge your claim. You are a son of Odin, a brother to Thor. Do you accept your kingship?"

"Aye."

"Do you swear to keep the old ways, to honor the gods, to sire children raised in the glory of Odin. Servants of truth. Protectors of Scandinavia?"

"Aye."

The priest set the crown on Thorolf's head. "Rise, King Thorolf of Borg."

"Odin bless the king," his captains said.

"Now bring in the woman," the high priest ordered his attendants. "Lady Runa must meet her lord and his captains."

Chapter Thirty-One

RUNA'S STOMACH TIGHTENED as she walked behind the high priest's attendants, on her way to a meeting with Thorolf and his captains who just arrived from Borg. Thankfully, Haldana was permitted to join her. In fact, the woman held on to her arm, offering the support Runa needed. They entered the temple sanctuary, paused in front of the altar to pay respect to the gods, then continued down a narrow corridor where a dozen closed doors were.

Torches lined the stone walls, providing ample light. The attendants knocked on the fourth door and Runa thought she'd faint from nervous anticipation.

"Come in," a deep voice sounded from within.

Runa entered the chamber where she found Thorolf seated with five strangers standing beside him. The high priest lounged on a couch in the corner, drinking from a silver goblet.

"Close the door, Lady Runa," Thorolf said too formally. "My captains have come a long way to meet their future queen."

She gave Haldana a helpless look before she shut the door, left alone with these men.

"Welcome," the high priest smiled at her. "It has been a while since we last talked. I trust you are comfortable staying with Haldana and the other women?"

"Aye," she said. "Though I prefer the privacy of my own

space."

"Spoken like a woman who knows what she wants and deserves," the priest chuckled. "After tonight, you will have all the privacy you require."

"Lady Runa," Thorolf spoke.

She turned to him and curtsied, marveling at the crown on his head. "You've claimed your kingdom?"

"Aye. There was no reason to delay. I am glad you are here, sweet one." He motioned for her to step closer. "I want to introduce you to Captain Dreng first."

"Tis an honor," the soldier said, bowing. "Words cannot describe how it feels to know King Thorolf will have such a beautiful and capable lady at his side. May Frigg grant you happiness and many children."

"Thank you, Sir," she said, offering her hand to the captain. He took it and plied a soft kiss to her fingers. "I hope your journey here was uneventful."

The captains were all dressed in similar fashion; black tunics and braies, copper beads decorated the ends of the braids in their beards, silver bracelets and rings on their wrists and fingers, and fur cloaks.

"We were delayed by a snowstorm, otherwise, peaceful."

Thorolf made the rest of the introductions, each warrior as respectful and charming as the next. If these were the men tasked with safeguarding Thorolf and seeing his will done in Borg, she knew he would succeed at whatever he did. Her greatest concern was whether they would accept her or not. Would the people of Borg welcome her as their queen?

Tales about the northlands had been whispered in her ears from a young age. The land of giants veiled by mist, snow, and ice. Allfather was even rumored to walk openly among these ancient people. And though the Trondelag had its own appealing lore, her brothers and their warriors paled in comparison to these behemoths.

"I require some time alone with my betrothed," he said.

The high priest and captains were quick to respond, leaving the solar.

Thorolf stood then and closed the distance between them. "I've waited days to see you like this." He tried to hug her, but Runa stepped out of reach.

"Waited? Or conveniently forgot about me?"

Thorolf looked completely baffled. "Never," he denied. "You are the reason I am standing here now, reunited with my men and wearing this crown."

She sniffled, touched by his words but doubting herself. "I am overjoyed for you, Thorolf. Believe me, I am. However, the man I fell in love with is no longer here. He disappeared the moment the high priest reminded you of your true identity."

"The high priest didn't remind me of anything. I carried that secret around year after year, burdened by it. He insisted I accept the truth. Take back what was mine."

A desperate need filled her. "I never wish to be a hardship, an obligation you cannot escape."

"Runa…" This time he didn't give her a choice. Thorolf swept her off her feet and carried her to the couch. He sat down and balanced her on his knees. "Look at me."

Tears blurred her vision, but she tried to meet his steady gaze.

"What nonsense have those temple maidens been filling your head with?'

"N-nothing at all. Only the truth about my misdirected passion to join their order. I romanticized my childish dream as any inexperienced girl does. My eyes are open now, Thorolf. Not only to this place, but the life I might not have becoming your wife."

He thumbed a stray tear off her cheek. "Not have? I don't understand."

"I never wish to become an afterthought."

He frowned, cupped her face between both palms, and kissed her gently. "You think I'd forget you? Lock you away as some bastard husbands do once a woman has given him children? Is this your honest opinion of me, Runa?"

"I-I...."

"Have I given you reason to question my intentions? To doubt my affection and love?"

"No."

"To cast me into the same pile of filth that some men deserve to be put in? Faithless swine that they are?"

"Never." He sounded so angry and she immediately regretted sharing her deepest worries. Thorolf would naturally hate anyone disloyal—his uncle betrayed him in the worst way, leaving him an orphan with no home. Thorolf needed her to love him, to restore his faith in family. "Forgive me. I couldn't see past my own fear. Everything has happened so quickly. And there's the question of my maid's whereabouts and Prince Axel. I mourn their loss. I am a prisoner of my own guilt."

"This is all that matters to me, Runa." He laced his fingers with hers, then moved their hands over his pounding heart. "The source of my lifeblood. It beats for you. *Only you.*"

She believed him.

"Never let anything come between us. I'd rather you ask me a question than hold the negative emotions inside until your doubt festers into something more destructive. I am always here for you, Runa." He stood with her in his arms and she clung to his neck, her head resting against his broad chest.

Their gazes locked in unspoken passion. She could see and

feel the love radiating from his body. Then he deposited her on the edge of the couch and crouched at her feet.

"You were my queen long before today," he declared, his warm fingers sliding up her legs underneath her skirt. "The only woman I've ever loved."

She spread her thighs and relaxed against the back of the couch, letting him touch her—hoping he'd take her now.

Thorolf shoved her skirt above her knees and Runa lifted her hips so he could expose her torso. The moment his soft lips made contact with her core, she arched her neck, sighing in utter pleasure. It had been too long since he'd touched her this way. His thick, strong fingers she'd grown to love thrust inside of her demandingly.

"Come for me, Runa," he growled, licking her again. "Now."

Merciless, his tongue and fingers circled over her flesh. He nipped the sensitive spot that made her see stars whenever she peaked, adding another finger to torture her with, filling her completely.

"Thorolf," she moaned. "Please…"

He gazed up at her. "I will do things to you tomorrow night you will never forget. After our vows." Then he slid up her body and captured her mouth savagely. As their tongues tangled together, she tasted her own body and it excited her.

"I want to hear you groan with pleasure, Runa." The kisses deepened as he stroked her between the legs with more urgency.

"I-I love you," she whispered between shallow breaths, the faint throb of ecstasy building.

"Aye," he hissed. "And I love you, my queen."

She couldn't hold back any longer. She dug her fingernails into the sides of his head, pulling him closer, wishing he could climb inside her body and never leave. She burst and Thorolf stopped moving and closed his eyes as she throbbed around his fingers.

"Tis wonderful," she murmured once she caught her breath.

"Aye," he agreed. "A gift from the gods we must never take for granted. I will have you this way every night, Runa. Spread beneath me. I will never give you another chance to doubt my feelings. And this..." He pulled back just enough so he could caress her belly. "I will keep filled with our treasured babes."

Everything she ever wanted in this world sat before her. There was no room left in her heart for confusion. What she missed growing up, her mother and love from her father, shouldn't dominate her thoughts or make her doubt the possibility of gaining true contentment. They'd forge their own future. Have many sons and daughters. Win the hearts of their people, together. Thorolf loved her *and* she loved him. Until Ragnarok came and, quite possibly, long after.

Chapter Thirty-Two

THE NEXT EVENING, Thorolf wondered if any man could be more fortunate than him. Riveted by Runa's ethereal beauty, the silvery-green gown she wore, and the splendor of the sanctuary, he felt unworthy. The room had been decorated with hundreds of lit candles, evergreen wreaths, and colorful ribbons. The warmth and joy inside made him forget the bitter cold of winter.

Fifteen temple maidens preceded Runa down the main aisle of the chamber, holding a single candle, heads bowed in reverence to the gods. As each one approached the altar where Thorolf waited with the high priest, they curtsied and then formed a semicircle to the left of the dais. Finally, after the last maiden moved aside, Thorolf fully beheld his bride—a radiant smile on her lips. He stretched his hand out and she took it, her eyes focused solely on him.

"Lady Runa," the high priest greeted her.

"Sir." She curtsied.

"Are you ready to begin King Thorolf? Lady Runa?"

"Aye," they answered together.

"The light and hope in this world is never more pronounced than when a man and maid find love. True love. And when the gods bless the union, the celebration is that much sweeter. King Thorolf of Borg and Lady Runa of the Trondelag are the blessed recipients of such a rare gift."

Thorolf turned slightly, taking Runa's other hand in his.

"Though the circumstances surrounding the way these two found each other sadden us, from the ashes, hope is reborn. Lives were lost to protect the innocent. And those men will never be forgotten."

"King Thorolf and Lady Runa, do you recognize the supremacy of Odin, pledge faith in the gods, swear allegiance to each other, forsaking all others—even to death."

Thorolf squeezed Runa's tiny hands. "Aye. Until Allfather demands my life."

"Lady Runa?"

"Aye. Until Allfather demands my life."

"Kneel before the altar," the priest directed.

Thorolf waited for her to settle on the silk pillow first, then started to lower himself.

"In the name of Odin," a deep voice boomed, "What are you doing with my sister?"

Thorolf regained his balance and swung around, finding Jarl Roald and thirty of his best warriors standing at the back of the sanctuary. "Roald," he said, hoping to make peace with his new brother-in-law before violence broke out.

"Roald?" he hissed, stalking forward. "Is this how you address your master? Weeks away from home have made you forget your place, Captain Thorolf. I am sure I can help you remember."

Murmurs sounded from below.

"Jarl Roald," the high priest interjected, stepping off the raised stage. "I expected your arrival days ago."

Roald smirked. "Even I am not capable of controlling the weather, Priest."

The high priest nodded. "Even so, I could not delay the

ceremony any longer. I am sure you will find everything in order. This marriage will benefit your family and the temple."

"How so? Runa was meant to wed a man of wealth and rank, not a common soldier." Roald came even closer to the dais.

Thorolf clenched his fists at his sides, reminding himself that his former lord didn't know who or what he was. "I am no longer your servant or a soldier."

"No?" Roald looked about. "You can dress in fine robes and walk about this place like a king, but when you strip yourself naked at night, you will still be the man I know—a fatherless bastard who took advantage of my sister and betrayed my trust."

At those belittling words, Thorolf's captains surged forward, weapons drawn, surrounding him like a defensive wall.

"Please," the high priest said. "There is no need for bloodshed or insults. Jarl Roald is unaware of who he addresses."

"The only person I wish to speak with is my sister. Runa! Come down here."

Thorolf turned to his beloved bride. "Do you wish to talk to him?"

"Aye. He deserves to hear the truth."

"Very well. We will go together."

Hand-in-hand, Thorolf guided Runa around his men until they stood a few feet away from her enraged brother. "Speak your words, Jarl Roald."

"Runa," Roald muttered. "What is this? Why have you agreed to marry this man? I gave you every consideration. Trusted you. You were headed to Prince Axel's home."

She swallowed, her body shaking a bit, but not afraid to meet her brother's gaze. "I never intended to marry Prince Axel, Roald. Surely you knew it."

"Aye. The moment you left home I knew you had lied to

me. But how could I recall you without insulting Axel? I hoped you'd change your mind and realize what a good man he was. But I see the poor prince never had a chance. Thorolf saw to it, I'm sure."

Roald's accusatory tone angered Thorolf. He let go of Runa's hand and pushed her behind him. "Speak plainly."

"You claim Jarl Skrymir murdered Axel's men and mine. Why do you still live? Where is the prince's body? Are there any other witnesses?"

"Jarl Roald..." The high priest stepped between the men. "You will address King Thorolf with respect. The same honor you demand for yourself. I assure you the king harmed no one. He was a victim of Skrymir's treachery as much as your sister was. Both sought safety within these walls and both shall have it."

"What did you call him?"

"King Thorolf of Borg."

"Runa?"

"It is true, Roald. There is much to tell, but not here, not in front of the guests."

Roald glared at Thorolf, his narrowed gaze wandering up his body and stopping on the crown atop his head. "You are the rumored lost son?"

"Aye."

"Shite!" Roald raked his fingers through his hair. "Why did you hide it?"

"There are many reasons. Some known, others will stay a secret and follow me to the grave."

"And this?" Roald motioned between Thorolf and Runa. "How long has this relationship been going on? Have you spoiled my sister? Is she pregnant? Is that the reason for this rushed ceremony?"

"Bite your tongue, Roald." Thorolf had heard enough. He gripped Roald by the front of his tunic, ready to shake the life out of him. "Never insult my bride."

"She is *my* sister," Roald spit, burying his fist in Thorolf's shirt. "And from what I heard, not yet your wife. I arrived in time to stop this wedding. She will accompany me home."

"No." Thorolf gave him a teeth-rattling shake. Though taller and heavier than Roald, Thorolf knew how fearless his former lord was. He had won Thorolf's admiration long ago. None of that mattered now. If he tried to take Runa away, he'd kill the man.

"Stop it!" Runa flung herself at them, tears in her eyes. "Leave him alone, Roald." She slapped at her brother's fisted hand. "Let me be happy. Let me be loved for the first time in my life. Why would you care where I ended up? Did the gods not bless you with a wife and children already? And Konal? I am nothing to you."

Roald's mouth opened and he slowly let go of Thorolf's tunic. "Nothing to me? Where did you get that idea? Who told you I didn't love you?"

"You did, a hundred times. With every disapproving stare, every frown, every time you refused to hug or kiss me, or listen to what I had to say."

"Damn you," he muttered. "Damn me for never realizing it."

His posture changed and Thorolf signaled for his captains to stand down. "If you will give us your blessing, Jarl Roald, I will work hard to make your sister the happiest woman alive. And I will sign a treaty with you, guaranteeing our partnership in trade and war. My sword is yours. My friendship and respect unwavering."

Roald's gaze lingered on Thorolf for a long moment before

he looked at Runa again. "He is the man you love?"

"Aye."

"You wish to be a queen?"

"I am still struggling with the idea."

Roald gave her a sad smile. "Borg is far away, Runa. Tis like a different world."

"I know."

"Have you caught Jarl Skrymir?" he asked Thorolf. "I can taste his blood, I want revenge."

Thorolf understood that need. "Winter has hit hard in the high country. We search a wide area day and night hoping to find a trace of the bloody bastard. We've had no luck. As soon as the snow melts, I will gather my best men and make war on his mountain stronghold and strip away everything he holds dear."

"I, too, pledge my army," Roald said, offering his arm.

"Add a hundred men from the temple guard," the high priest said as Thorolf clutched his brother-in-law's forearm in friendship and peace.

"I swear before Odin," Thorolf said.

"You have my blessing, Runa."

"I do?" She couldn't believe it. Roald had never given in to anything so easily. "Truly?"

"Aye."

She rushed into her brother's loving embrace. "Thank you, Roald. I will make you proud of me someday."

"I already am." He lifted her chin and stared into her eyes. "Now hurry, before I change my mind."

Chapter Thirty-Three

After a very intoxicated Roald had stumbled over to give his sister a last kiss before he went to bed and the high priest had gifted his new wife with a pair of gold goblets to carry to her new home in Borg, that's when Thorolf could no longer wait to get his bride alone. He'd shared her enough. Watched her sip her wine, play with the meat and vegetables on her trencher, and offer smiles to every stranger that came forward to meet the new queen.

"I've been patient, Wife," he whispered in her ear.

"Oh?" she asked, an attractive blush rose in her cheeks.

"Very."

"Surely you can tolerate a little more, we will never have another night like this again. We get one wedding celebration and a lifetime of joy together."

"I disagree." Thorolf nibbled on the side of her neck. "We get one wedding night—which will lead to a lifetime of happiness."

"You've made this claim many times over the last couple of weeks, but I have nothing to compare it to. I must place my blind trust in you. Would you do the same, Husband?" She arched a brow in challenge.

"I'll always follow you, Runa. Eyes wide open or as a blind as an old woman. Tell me what your heart desires at this very moment, I will give it to you as a bride gift."

"Anything?"

"Aye."

"Purchase the temple maiden, Haldana's freedom from the high priest and the guard named Balfer. Let them journey to Borg with us and start a new life."

Thorolf couldn't help but chuckle at his wife's cleverness. "You tricked me, Runa." He admired the delicate circlet of gold on her head, embellished with amber and a single ruby at the center—the crown that belonged to his mother. "Spoken like a true queen."

"Will you do it?"

"Temple maidens are as sacred as oaths. It will take more than a king's share of gold to buy her freedom."

"I understand," she said as she unclasped the gold choker around her neck and dropped it on the table in front of him. "This should cover her ransom, no?"

"You'd trade your mother's necklace for the woman?"

"More if I had all my jewels here."

"She means that much to you?"

Runa nodded. "The friend I always wished for. And the soldier is her lover."

"If the high priest knew of her infidelity, he'd slit her throat."

"All the more reason to rescue her from this place. Though I respect what the temple symbolizes, I will never ask to come here again. I've been wrong all of my life, Thorolf, so determined to live here and serve Odin. I will fulfill my duty by giving you sons who will take up the sword in Allfather's name."

Thorolf leaned close to his wife. "Are you prepared to do so tonight? I wish to put a babe inside your belly now."

She shivered, gooseflesh appearing on her slender arms. "Whatever you wish, my lord."

He growled, pleased by her response. "I will free the woman and her lover."

"Thank you." She covered his hand with hers.

"Now, we will excuse ourselves from the hall." He stood and scooped her into his arms.

The remaining guests hooted and clapped their hands, raising their cups in salute.

A bridal chamber had been prepared for them on the other side of the sanctuary. He carried his precious bride out of the longhouse and across the way, entering the sanctuary and not giving a damn if the gods expected him to stop and give thanks. Tonight belonged to him, to them. His body hummed with desire and lust as he got closer to their room.

Once inside, he bolted the door, locking the world out.

Though small, the space was luxurious, complete with a wide bed and a large brazier to keep warm by. A small feast of wine, cheese, bread, and smoked fish had been prepared and set out on the table. And Runa's trunks had been moved over from the temple maidens' house. He set her on her feet, giving her a moment to get accustomed to their new surroundings.

She sidled up to the bed, running her fingers over the linens and furs. "Where did all of this come from?" She looked over at him. "I'm sure the priests can afford such rich things, but to provide them for their guests?"

"I purchased them for you."

"How?"

"From the gold I've saved over the years, Runa. I'm a man of simple needs."

"Your generosity leaves me speechless. Thank you, Thorolf."

He went to her, hugging her from behind, his hungry fingers tracing her lush curves, claiming her full breasts. She leaned into him, his erection poking her in the back. There'd be no hiding his excitement, not that he needed to anymore. She belonged to him. His very own wife. His queen and lover.

"Do you know how long I loved you from a distance? How many times I wanted to grab you up and kiss you? Spank you for being insolent?" he asked, massaging her shoulders.

"Did you know I felt the same? That every man I met failed to impress me because I always compared them to you? They weren't tall enough or muscular enough. Their eyes were too close together or the wrong color. They weren't honorable and kind like you've always been." She turned in his arms, reaching up and locking her fingers behind his neck. "You are the most handsome man I've ever seen."

"Am I now?" he teased.

"And the biggest." Her hand slid between his legs and cupped the painful lump in his braies.

He groaned, wanting to get her naked. "Runa…"

"Shhh." She held a finger to his lips. "I know what you want, Husband."

She retreated a couple steps and started to untie the laces at her back. He watched in silent fascination as she slid out of her gown and removed her veil and slippers. She stood before him as proud as any queen should be and Thorolf loved her more in that moment than ever before. Though innocent, she possessed the uninhibited confidence of an experienced woman. The kind of woman made to please him forever.

"Will you do the same for me?" she asked.

"You want me to strip for you?"

"Aye," she said. "I want to see your body, to enjoy it as much as you have mine."

Seconds later, he gave her what she wanted, standing naked in the soft candlelight, waiting for her to finish exploring his body with her hungry eyes. "Do I please you, Runa?'

"You are truly magnificent, Thorolf. May I see your backside?"

He held in the laugh that threatened to escape as he turned around. In no way did he want to discourage her. This boldness would see her through the pinch of pain she'd feel when he first entered her. Then he'd make passionate love to her all night.

He shivered when her cool hands ran up his back. "Why are you so firm and I am soft?"

"Allfather intended it that way," he answered.

Continuing her close scrutiny of his form, Thorolf nearly yelped when she ran a finger up the crack of his arse. He spun around. "Are you satisfied, my love?"

"No," she said softly. "But I am willing to wait."

"I'm not." He took hold of her wrist and tugged her to the bed. They fell onto the mattress together, laughing and touching each other in earnest. Thorolf pinched one of her pebble-hard nipples, flicking his tongue over it again and again. She stiffened, letting out a small moan. "Aye," he sang out, lost in her softness and beauty. "Roll onto your back for me."

He climbed on top of her, his knees positioned on either side of her hips. With tender admiration, he cupped her breasts, lifting and squeezing them together, forming a tunnel where his face could fit perfectly. The ache in his groin increased tenfold as he licked and caressed her.

Then he brushed his thumb lightly over her lips, enjoying the way her pink tongue circled around his fingers, tasting and tempting him. Leaving him more vulnerable than he'd ever been on a battlefield, his heart wide open and receptive for the first time in ten years.

He moved up her body and lifted her arms above her head, dipping down so he could capture that sweet mouth, inhaling her lips and tongue. She writhed beneath him, as restless and desperate as he was. Perhaps it was time. He'd prepared her for this moment. Spoke frankly with her about what to expect.

"Do you want me inside you, Runa?" He released her hands.

She smiled.

"Do you know what you were made for?" he asked, positioning his manhood at her entrance, feeling the heat and wetness with his fingers. "For me, my love. You were made for me."

He thrust, her tight muscles gripping his length. Arching his back, he closed his eyes and waited for the initial shock of being inside her to pass. She whimpered and clawed at his shoulders, urging him to continue. But Thorolf questioned his stamina for a few heartbeats. The reality of where he was, married to the woman he'd loved for so long—fantasized about bedding and possessing threatened to make him explode inside her.

"What is it?" she whispered, cupping his cheek.

He stared into her green eyes, wide and expressive, filled with awe and love for him.

"I-I needed a moment to recover, sweetling, nothing more." He lowered himself completely, skin-to-skin with her.

She wiggled her hips and Thorolf moved with renewed confidence, sliding in and out of her, loving the way her expressions changed with each thrust. He'd finally marked her, claimed her, loved her with everything he had to give.

When he could no longer control himself, they whispered each other's names as pleasure mutually rolled over them—the night still very young and their desire only momentarily satisfied.

Chapter Thirty-Four

THREE DAYS LATER, Runa trekked outside in the fresh snow, dressed in new furs and boots, ready to make the journey to her new home in Borg. Thorolf had kept his word, Haldana and her lover had been released from service to the high priest for a generous donation to the temple coffers. Already settled on her mount, Haldana grinned as Runa approached the horse, waiting for her.

"Tis a beautiful morning," the maid said.

"Aye," Runa agreed. "How many days' ride is it to Borg?"

"Three," Haldana answered. "It is worth the effort. You will see some of the most beautiful sights on the way."

Runa handed her maid a couple packages to tuck in her saddle bags and then went to search for her brother among the many soldiers packing their gear. She passed by Captain Harald and his family, yet another joyous ending. They gladly accepted Thorolf's offer to relocate.

Finding Roald a few yards away, she called out to him. "Jarl Roald. Were you going to leave without saying goodbye to your sister?"

He chuckled. "And miss kissing the only queen I personally know?"

The title would take some getting used to. "I would have sent my army after you."

He finished securing his weapons on his horse and faced her. "You have an army at your disposal now? How quickly you've adapted to your new life, Runa. I am happy for you. Proud and maybe a little bit envious of the great adventure you are about to embark on."

"Truly?" Runa couldn't imagine her brother being jealous of her. But even if he was just teasing, she liked this new side of Roald.

He stepped in front of her and gripped her arms. "Our mother and father would praise your courage, Runa. You've done your duty—married a man of high morals and rank. Secured an alliance for our family. And most important, fallen in love. A rare accomplishment for any young woman."

"I only followed your example, Brother. Accepted a man who I thought didn't have anything in this world to offer but his heart. Look how generously the gods have rewarded us for taking a leap of faith. You have Eva and the twins. Konal has Silvia and their son. And now I have King Thorolf—the only man I could ever love."

"And he has you, Runa. Never doubt your value. I know you were very young when Mother died, but you are so much like her. Intelligent, generous, and beautiful."

Runa tried to blink the tears away. Why hadn't they made peace like this before? "Your kind words will stay with me forever."

"As should this." He reached inside his cloak and revealed the gold choker Runa had given to Thorolf to purchase Haldana's freedom.

"Where did you get it?"

"Thorolf gave it to me."

Runa bowed her head, afraid Roald would be angry that she was willing to give away a treasure their mother had bequeathed to her.

"Why hang your head, Queen Runa? You chose to value a human life over a piece of jewelry. For that, I wish to return the necklace. Keep it close to your heart. Our mother often said a family is what you make it. I believe you will rise to that challenge more than any of us could. Look about, Runa, you've already started to gather loyal subjects. Captain Harald and his family love you. Haldana and her captain would die for you. Thorolf's men worship you. Stand tall and proud."

She threw herself at Roald and he caught her. "I love you, Roald."

"What is this?" He held her away from him and wiped the tears from her cheeks. "I will see you in early spring. Together, Thorolf and I will hunt Skrymir down and kill him. If Prince Axel and your maid yet live, they will be freed."

"Aye," she said. "But will you set me free, too?"

Roald had fire in his eyes, like she'd shattered the moment of happiness between them. "The fate-binding?"

"Please," she begged. "I will never be completely at peace unless you remove it. Konal's future should not depend on me." Truth hit her hard. The fate-binding had never been about her at all. Roald didn't want Konal to leave home, to establish his own steading, and become a jarl. "You cannot make him stay, Roald. Let us all go. We will love you that much more for it, believe me."

Thorolf joined them. "It is time, Runa."

"Wait," she said. "Roald isn't finished with me yet."

"There isn't a better place to remove the fate-binding," he commented. "Odin will stand as my witness. I free you, Queen Runa. I absolve any responsibility you have for the wellbeing of our brother, Konal the Red. Let his fate be separate. And may you live a long and happy life." He kissed the top of her head, turned, and trudged away.

"He is a complicated man," Runa mumbled.

"Tis a family trait," Thorolf said. "I sympathize with him. He's lost as much as you. Maybe more because he is the eldest and responsible for all of you. He'll recover in time. Now, come with me. I am anxious to leave this place and see our home."

Runa took her husband's hand and faced the temple one last time. "I never thought the night I came here seeking aid that I'd end up here with you. I honestly thought you were dead and my only hope was to join the maidens."

He tucked Runa in his arms, holding her close. "The gods had other plans, my love."

"Aye," she said, hoping those plans included many healthy children and a long life with her beloved husband. "Praise great Odin. Creator and master of all things."

"Hail great Odin," Thorolf said with a wicked smile. "Trickster and womanizer. A god with a heart the size of all of Scandinavia, because he gave you to me."

They walked to their horses and Thorolf helped her up, giving her hand a little squeeze before he left her and climbed atop his own mount. He twisted in the saddle and gazed at the large company of people waiting for his command. "To Borg," he said, then tapped his horse's sides with his heels, more than ready to go home.

THE END

Made in the USA
Columbia, SC
06 October 2021

46832432R00115